DONE
P9-BYB-316

Guns of Arizona

Center Point
Large Print

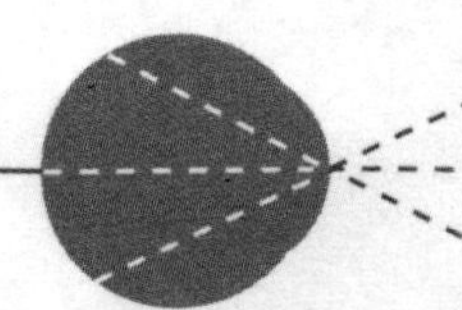

This Large Print Book carries the
Seal of Approval of N.A.V.H.

Guns of Arizona

LAURAN PAINE

CENTER POINT PUBLISHING
THORNDIKE, MAINE

This Center Point Large Print edition
is published in the year 2006 by arrangement with
Golden West Literary Agency.

The text of this Large Print edition is unabridged. In other aspects, this book may vary from the original edition. Printed in Thailand. Set in 16-point Times New Roman type.

ISBN: 1-58547-855-5
ISBN 13: 978-1-58547-855-2

Library of Congress Cataloging-in-Publication Data

Paine, Lauran.
Guns of Arizona / Lauran Paine.--Center Point large print ed.
p. cm.
ISBN 1-58547-855-5 (lib. bdg. : alk. paper)
1. Cattle drives--Fiction. 2. Arizona--Fiction. 3. Large type books. I. Title.

PS3556.A34G848 2006
813'.54--dc22

2006014058

ONE

McCarty wore a broadcloth suit and starched white shirt. Across his vest the gold links of his heavy watch-chain moved from his pleasure and his rough breathing. He said with grave formality, "Ma'm; you're exactly what this ranch has needed for twenty years." Then McCarty stiffly bobbed up and down from the waist and departed the room, rolling along with the precision and awesome majesty of a dreadnought.

For Jane Adair as well as for the three big and vital men in that candlelit dining-room, McCarty's approval of Jane clinched it, for Jeb McCarty had been cook, laundress, mother and *majordomo* of this Arizona household for precisely as long as he'd said the Morgan Ranch had been without a woman—twenty years.

Jeb was a medium-sized man but in the company of old Hyatt Morgan and his two sons he seemed much smaller, for all the Morgan men were well over six feet tall, rangy and rawboned, heavy-built and as solid as stone. As unmoving too, it had been said down around Tucson, some seven miles southward.

Lex was the eldest of Hyatt's sons; he was in his middle thirties, a handsome, bronzed man with a strong face and a jaw of iron. Lex had never, for some reason, married, and he sat across the dining-room table now gazing upon Jane Adair with a strange expression, part wonderment, part wistfulness.

Lex was most like old Hyatt; if he had something to say he said it, if he didn't he was silent. His fists were respected on the range as well as in Tucson, and his gunmanship was also respected. Yet Lex Morgan was not ordinarily a troublesome man. He was at times seemingly humorless, reticently taciturn and inward, but usually that was only when women were around, like now, and it gave people an impression of big Lex Morgan which was actually quite erroneous.

On the other hand Ward Morgan, old Hyatt's youngest, was transparent as branch-water. When he smiled he put one in mind of a pleased puppy. When he laughed the roundabout world seemed suddenly to be a much better place. Unlike Lex and Hyatt, young Ward was dark like his mother had been, with liquid brown eyes and tight-clinging curly black hair. Those who remembered back twenty years and more down in Tucson said the mother of Lex and Ward had been Spanish, and as rumor often does, it had her coming directly from Aramayona in Spain and alternatively from the governor's Palace in Province Sonora.

Ward could easily have been descended from Spain's iron *Conquistadores;* except for his out-sized bigness, patently a legacy from old Hyatt Morgan, he rode as only Spaniards could ride and he laughed with a quick flash of even white teeth. His moods, not quite mercurial, were nonetheless reminiscent of a different remembering blood from the same blood of his grizzled father and his sometimes unfathomable brother.

It was probably this difference which had initially attracted Jane Adair to Ward Morgan. The first time she'd seen him enter Tucson he had been riding a fine black horse at the head of the Morgan *vaqueros,* six of those indigenous swarthy and sturdy Arizonans of Mexican descent who were so different from their ragged and oftentimes treacherous cousins across the border.

Ward had seemed then to be the epitome of everything a girl's heart desired; young, very handsome, vital and masculinely compelling. She had accepted his contrived introduction through friends as a reciprocal interest, which it had been, and for two years now she and Ward Morgan had been keeping steady company.

And yet, because Ward had known it would be so, he had told her they'd have to observe a rigorous protocol. Old Hyatt would never approve of nor accept a girl in his house whom he considered undecorous. So, after two years, this was the gratifying result; she was at the great oaken dining table of Hyatt Morgan and his stalwart sons at the huge Morgan ranch in a setting which had taken the best of two worlds, Spanish and American, blended it into the unique courtliness which was so basically Arizonan, and now lavished its stylized formality upon her.

At twenty, Jane Adair was more woman than girl. She had thick masses of wavy red-gold hair. The candlelight got snared in it and writhed in shades of nearly darkest copper when she moved. Her eyes were as grey as a wintry day, or as smoke rising from an oak-fire against a leaden sky. They were large, set well apart and had a way of looking directly at a person. They were eyes that held a smoky depth of passion or a slate-grey coldness. Her mouth was long and curved and full at the center. It was lying gently closed now with a faint-hinting lilt at the outer corners. It was the rich, ripe mouth of a woman and not the pliable, soft and willing mouth of a girl. But if those three strongly admiring men saw this, or even understood that this was so, they seemed not to care, for with this beautiful woman among them in their womanless world, each of them was gallant, each was lifted by her presence to his individual plane. Even old Hyatt, grey and grizzled, as hard as iron and as uncompromising as the night, seemed different in this magic setting of age-darkened furniture, candlelight, and the vital presence of a beautiful woman. He seemed old enough to be concerned for her welfare yet young enough to respond in a purely masculine way to her loveliness.

When McCarty brought the supper Hyatt lifted an etched glass half-full of blood-red wine, gallantly tipped it and said: "To beauty and goodness. To Miss Jane Adair."

"To beauty," echoed Lex, gazing steadily over.

Ward flashed his magic smile, rolled a passionately claiming look around at Jane Adair and stood up. Those three big men drank with candlelight touching their hawk-like, somehow alike, somehow quite different, faces, and sat back down.

Jane's eyes glowed; for the daughter of a village schoolmaster in a border country as indifferent to formal education as Tucson was, this was a far cry from her humble beginnings in this raw land. To her this was an altogether different world; here were stalwart, hard men who met life head-on. These were the real rulers of this immense and often violent land, these big, capable, fearless men in their massive adobe hacienda with their fiercely loyal *vaqueros* in the middle of thousands of acres of cattle country.

Her father, dead one year now from the lung-fever which had brought him here with his motherless daughter from Massachusetts, had often told her that in Southern Arizona it helped if a man's heritage was good, but most important, if the man had it in him to be great, this was the land for that greatness to come out; here, he'd said, in his soft yet convincing manner, was a world waiting for strong masters. Here, nature drew forth from men whatever was in them to make them great or small, powerful or mean, courageous or cowardly.

What he'd never had time to tell her because he didn't know of her interest in young Ward Morgan before his death at forty-four, was that the successful in this land had to also be as uncompromising, as hard and often as cruel, as this great and empty land also was; that survival mattered more than progress, that strength had to exist equally in the woman as in the men, and that this ancient place would destroy those who would coerce it exactly as it had destroyed the

Spanish for bringing civilization to a hushed world which had been ancient out of mind before the first Spaniard, the first Apache, the first biped of any kind, ever damned a creek, cut down a tree, or splashed across the sluggish Santa Cruz River which rolled muddily southward arrow-straight down into Mexico.

Still, sitting in the solid splendor of that candlelit dining-room now, she could sense some of this, for the Morgan men, although dressed in white shirts and suit-coats tonight, nevertheless had about them the aura of guns and horses and blazing suns. Night nor the three-foot-thick walls closing fortress-like around her, could entirely keep out the inherent perils and the conflicting purposes of the outside world, not even in the darkness, because, day or night, the silence was always there, and it was this endless stillness that never let anyone in Southern Arizona forget that life here was very real and very basic; people did what they had to do in order to survive. The silence said that, the night said it, and the kind of leashed violence lying latent in the eyes of the Morgans, even tonight, proved it.

Three years in Tucson had given her some vague notion of these underlying things, but, being a woman just past being a girl, the harshness and the violence were always just beyond arms' reach, and she was content to leave it like that, so, when old Hyatt turned his sun-layered and forthright features towards her and smiled, she smiled back.

He said, "Young lady, it does my son proud to know

you. It's been a long time since anyone like you has come here." The old man's steely eyes turned smoky, his voice lowered a notch. "Jeb is right; twenty years is too long a time."

He was thinking back to another woman and another time with the visible pain these thoughts brought to him unashamedly apparent.

Ward said quietly, "Jeb's always right, paw," and with this statement turned the old man's thoughts away from sadness.

"He is for a fact, Ward." Old Hyatt threw his youngest son an assenting look, then returned his attention to Jane Adair. "Jeb rode into this country with me longer ago than I like to remember. He helped me raise my boys, build my ranch, and I guess he even deserves more credit for some of these things than I do. When I went east after cattle he ran the ranch."

"And the boys," said Ward lightly, then grinned. "And Jane I don't mean he just ruled us either, I mean he literally *ran* us—with a switch sometimes, with his rawhide quirt other times. How about it, Lex?"

The older brother's eyes softly shone as he quietly smiled over at Jane Adair, and nodded, but did not speak.

"Well; it didn't hurt you any," said old Hyatt. "And I've got a notion he looked the other way a good many times too. Like the time you two were ganglin' lads an' caught that Apache hidin' in the rocks to steal himself a horse."

Now Lex spoke up. His face quickly clouded and he

said rather hastily, as though to break up this conversation, “You wouldn’t know it now, Ma’m, but Jeb McCarty used to be one of the best *vaqueros* in Southern Arizona. He could throw a sixty foot riata with the best of the Mexicans and he could cook up a pot of peppered-beans—and eat them—without shedding one single tear; he’d deliberately make them so hot the *vaqueros* would gasp, and that, as you probably know, is not a small accomplishment, down here.”

Jane listened and she laughed when the others laughed, but she also wondered what Lex had prevented his father from relating. One thing she was certain of, as she watched powerful Lex Morgan: if he didn’t want to speak about something wild horses would not make him do so.

They talked after that back and forth, sometimes relating adventures, sometimes telling humorous things, but Lex never again took the initiative. He ate, and he gazed steadily across the table once in a while, but he only chuckled when it was appropriate to do so, or he smiled, but he let Ward and Hyatt do most of the talking, and in spite of herself, Jane Adair wondered about Lex Morgan. What was it that made him seem different from the others, but particularly different from young Ward.

It was more than their physical difference; it went deep down whatever it was. It was something inherent, something from their common sustaining environment which had formed Lex in a way different from Ward and even different from old Hyatt, even though these last two obviously had much in common otherwise. She couldn't prevent herself from being intrigued; Lex was in some ways a mystery and a challenge to her, and yet she now thought, as they sat there eating and talking, no matter how much a woman—any woman—was around Lex Morgan, she would never really know him.

Time passed, they finished supper, the men smoked and McCarty brought Jane Adair a surprise—genuine strawberry shortcake. In a land where nine-tenths of the people had never tasted a strawberry, this was old Jeb's eloquent way of expressing complete approval. Jane understood and her eyes misted.

TWO

They had to move seven hundred head of cattle ten miles westward as the spring grass strengthened. It was a custom encouraged by experience; in the spring and early summer-time the desert Apaches did not concentrate their raids around Tucson. They went racing down into Mexico which was their traditional plundering grounds. But later on, when the range dried, that sulphurous sun cowed the land with its pitiless blasting and the Mexicans stopped riding out with their caravans and remained listlessly in their towns, the Apaches returned to their homeland. That was when they turned to raiding at home, and that was why the Morgans, like all knowledgeable cattlemen in this wild land, grazed their herds miles away in the springtime—so that when the Apache scourge began, they would have ample good cured grass on the home ranges where they could bring their herds back and keep a close watch on them.

The Indians though were seldom as one hundred per cent Apache as the soldiers at Fort Lowell or Whipple were. They were Mexican marauders, sometimes Barracks or Fort Crittenden farther south claimed they dressed as Apaches, sometimes openly plunderers from down in Province Sonora. The difference was that while the cowmen occasionally caught and executed Mexican raiders, the Army could not, without a lot of paper-work and diplomatic risk, kill anything but Apache raiders, so, by the special magic of distance and swift interment, Mexican marauders were shot, planted, and blandly written into Official Reports as Apache renegades killed while performing criminal practices. It was neat, efficient, and more important, quite acceptable. The trouble was that fifty years hence, and longer, historians would draw up thoroughly perplexed by a unique fact: the Army had, during the borderland tenure, officially killed nearly twice as many Apaches as the field censuses said ever existed.

But this factor did not bother Arizona's residents, townsmen or cattlemen, at that time, nor as a matter of fact did they anticipate it or even consider it important. A raider, whatever his racial affinity, was a raider. If he was caught—as with that skulking Apache Lex and Ward had spied hiding in the rocks—he was shot to death. He could be Apache, Mexican, American, or any one of the borderland mixtures commonly called 'breeds, but one thing was certain—he was killed without delay and without remorse.

So, when the Morgan men organized their westward drive to good springtime grass, old Hyatt, with a minimum of excuses, left Ward and Lex in charge of details, saddled up and rode on down to Tucson. He had it in mind to do a quite unusual thing; he meant to fetch back Jane Adair.

Hyatt had his reasons for this. For one thing, he knew it would add lightness to an otherwise monotonous affair. For another it would please his younger, who was in some ways dearer to him than his elder. And finally, in his own shrewd way, Hyatt wanted to see how this beautiful girl would handle herself among little hardships and privations. How her temper would react to endless days of dust, sweat, and monotony. How she would look and act after eight hours in the saddle or riding the wagon under a blasting sun, for if Ward married this girl, brought her to the Morgan ranch to rule as the only woman on the place, Hyatt wanted to be dead certain she would be equal to it.

He never once doubted that she'd come on the drive, and he was correct in this assumption. When he strode into Hugh Crawford's warehouse, with its pleasant fragrances from spices, cured salt meat, new print cloth and all the other trade goods stored here, where

Jane Adair worked as book-keeper, she met him with a smile and a grey-eyed level look.

He asked her if she'd like to see what life was like at Morgan Ranch and she didn't even hesitate. Even when he explained they might be gone ten days.

She said, "I'd love to, but first I'll have to ask Mister Crawford."

Old Hyatt made a deprecatory gesture with one gloved hand. "Never mind; I'll talk to Mister Crawford. You go on home and get ready. I'll meet you in front of the school-house in half an hour."

She was hesitant; jobs for women in Tucson were very scarce. Without this book-keeping employment she would be destitute. Hyatt saw her look of worry and understood it. "Never mind," he confided in a low tone. "In case you hadn't heard, I own part of this company."

She left then, excited as a girl, and Hyatt went in search of paunchy, fretful Hugh Crawford, whom he located tallying-in bags of Utah salt at his rearmost loading docks.

Hugh spied old Hyatt instantly and went ahead to meet him. They clasped hands. Hugh began an earnest recital about business accounts but Hyatt brushed this aside in that short. brusque manner he used towards most men.

"I want to take Miss Adair on a cattle drive," he said, and Hugh Crawford's gaze flickered, turned interested but guarded. "In case you didn't know, Hugh, my youngest wants to marry her."

Hugh evidently didn't know because his eyes sprang wide open. Hyatt saw this and narrowed his eyes in a thoughtful expression.

He said: "Hugh; around Tucson there's more gossip per square foot than anywhere I ever been. Ward and Miss Jane been keeping company nearly two years now, and if you hadn't heard, why then I expect you're workin' too hard down here at the warehouse."

"Oh, I'd heard they were keeping company, Hyatt," responded Crawford quickly, "but I didn't know it was that serious."

"It is. She was to dinner at the ranch last week. Now, I'd like a leave of absence for a couple weeks for her."

Hyatt gave no reason, which was typical of him; as a man accustomed to command, he seldom gave reasons, only orders. He stood there gazing quietly at Crawford and waiting.

"Of course, Hyatt. I'll put one of the clerks to making entries until she gets back."

"Thanks, Hugh," old Hyatt said in that same brisk and impersonal tone. "I'll fetch her back to town when we finish up." He dropped his gaze to the sheaf of limp papers in Crawford's hands. "By the way, is that Mormon salt you're unloading?"

"Yes. The Army complained about sand being in the Mex stuff we sold them last winter, so for a better price I've contracted for this Utah salt."

"Dangerous trip," commented old Hyatt, thinking of the dreary, deadly miles those salt wagons had traversed from Utah's salt beds.

Crawford slightly shrugged, saying nothing, but with obviously indifferent thoughts about that. His establishment would buy Utah salt; it was up to the Mormons to deliver it. Hyatt understood that little shrug and dryly said, "Yeah. Well; see you when we get back, Hugh."

Crawford nodded and stood a moment watching big Hyatt Morgan striding back up through the warehouse. From behind a man's rumbling call brought Hugh's attention around to other matters and he walked back towards the loading docks.

Hyatt returned to the saddle, eased around and rode up through town as far as the dilapidated board-and-bat school-house. Jane lived in one of the little one-room cabins at the back. Her dead father had not only supervised the building of that school-house but had been its first headmaster, which was, in the Town Council's view, a splendid title for a teacher—the only teacher in fact—because, with an inexpensive show of small respect, they hadn't had to pay him very much actual cash.

Jane was waiting beside an old horse, once the property of her father. She'd filled both saddlebags and there was even a Winchester carbine slung from beneath the *rosadero,* something old Hyatt viewed with approval but which he'd hardly expected a beautiful girl to put there.

She was wearing a pale tan blouse, a long, rusty-colored split riding skirt, and had her mass of auburn hair caught up at the back of her head by a little green ribbon. She was smiling and eager, clear-eyed and faintly flushed. In a word, he thought, as he reined up, she was beautiful.

He smiled down at her and cleared his throat. "We'll be gone maybe ten days," he said.

"I'm quite prepared, Mister Morgan."

"You deserve to know it's hot and dusty and . . . not exactly suited for womanfolk on the trail."

"And perhaps dangerous," she murmured, her smile fading a little, her steady, smoky gaze meeting his look head-on. She rose up, settled across leather and shortened her reins. She suspected why he'd invited her on this trip. She'd had half an hour to think about it since he'd walked into that warehouse south of town. She said, "This was my father's horse; he's old and . . ."

"We'll leave him at the ranch," interrupted old Hyatt, settling in the saddle. "You can have another horse." With this minor detail disposed of he said, "Got everything you'll need, ma'am?"

"I think so."

"Fine. Let's get back then."

They rode out of Tucson with the sun directly overhead, with the land lying drowsily peaceful all around, and with the distantly roundabout mountain peaks standing heat-hazed in the distance.

It was a silent ride, for the most part. Jane, busy with her private thoughts, offered little in the way of voluntary conversation, and old Hyatt, a man unaccustomed to small-talk, actually unable, as Lex also was, to engage in it without great effort, rode silently along. Just before they came in sight of the great, pale-trunked cottonwood trees that eternally shaded the Morgan Ranch buildings ahead, he said, "Ma'am, have you thought of going back to Massachusetts? I mean, there's little enough for a girl with your background out here. It's not an easy life, like in the east."

"I like it," she said simply and forthrightly. "I love desert nights and daytime distances. You're used to the desert, Mister Morgan, so possibly you don't see in it the same things I see. Wildness and lonely beauty. A kind of ancient sadness that reaches inside a person."

He rode along, listening, saying nothing for a long time. When a faint, high ring came down the clear air from up among those onward buildings where a *vaquero* struck a shoeing-anvil, he raised his eyes, looked far out and said, "Ward's mother used to write poetry about this country. Maybe some day I can show you some of it." He swung around, his expression gentled away from its customary hardness just for a little while. "She used to say practically the same things. She loved the clear nights and the returning grasses each spring. I reckon you'll stay, Miss Jane. If you feel that way, why, I expect you should stay."

They rode on into the yard where busy men were at work under the quiet supervision of big Lex and the garrulous stormings of old Jeb McCarty, who could speak Spanish better than nearly any of the six Morgan Ranch *vaqueros,* certainly more colorfully.

Ward was not in sight. He had gone out to fetch in the *remuda*—the herd of range horses from which they'd make their selection of which horses to take along.

Lex stood straight up over by the barn doorway when he saw his father ride in with Jane Adair. He stood like that until Jeb walked over, jostled him and growled, "Don't stare; it ain't polite. Now what the devil did he bring her out for on a busy day like this."

"To take her along, Jeb," said Lex softly, watching that pair of riders approach.

Jeb jumped as though stung. "*What!* Take a *girl* along on a cattle drive?"

"Well," responded Lex, looking around at the older man, "she's got a pair of full saddlebags and a rifle, Jeb. She wouldn't be just out for a pleasure ride rigged out like that."

Jeb squinted up his eyes and sucked back his lips in a strongly disapproving expression. He bristled, but he had nothing more to say as Hyatt came up and halted, nodded at those two standing there in the doorway, stepped down, stepped around, and offered his gloved hand for Jane Adair to also dismount. Then the old man turned. He knew Jeb McCarty as well as Jeb knew him, and right this minute old Jeb was indignant enough to spout off, so Hyatt, in his briskest voice, said, "Jeb, you got the wagon loaded; the teams picked out?"

"Wagon's loaded, yes," snapped McCarty. "Ward's fetchin' in the *remuda*." Then old Jeb turned his fierce eyes towards Jane, masked his disapproving look, made a bow from the waist that set his watchfob to quivering, and levered up a wide smile. "Almighty pleased to see you again, Ma'am," he said, with that awkward gallantry he felt sure was the way the 'best people' conducted themselves in mixed company. "Here, let me take your horse."

As Jeb moved ahead to take Jane's horse he fired another flinty stare at old Hyatt. It rolled off Lex's father like water off a duck's back.

Jane turned. The riders of Morgan Ranch were busy at several tasks around the yard. Some were checking saddles, hackamores, bridles. Some were carefully and solemnly cleaning weapons. One, stripped to the waist and dusky color in the shade of a blacksmith shed, was sweatily fitting new shoes to a big black gelding—the private animal of Hyatt Morgan.

Over near the storehouse stood a scarred old wagon. It had soiled canvas lying slack over big bows, giving it the appearance of a starved animal of some kind where the bows showed through canvas.

Lex said to his father that the herd was a mile out and gathered. Hyatt threw a speculative look at the overhead sun, dropping off westerly and reddening slightly now, in early afternoon, then nodded.

"Good. There's a moon tonight. We'll make Tanque Verde before midnight with any luck."

A solid reverberation gradually swelled in the still, hot atmosphere. The Mexicans heard it first and stepped forward gazing northward where a big cloud of desert dust jumped up to hang in the air.

"Caballos," one of them sang out, and flagged for the others to run corral-ward with him. *"Venga muchachas;* the horses are coming!"

THREE

Jane and Jeb McCarty stood in barn-shade watching as that flashing big band of sleek animals came charging through dazzling sunlight. The *vaqueros* ran out with Lex and Hyatt to form a hat-flagging line, diverting those free-running beasts into the immense Morgan Ranch network of pole corrals. It was a wild moment and a wilder scene. Men called out, sometimes in English but mostly in Spanish, dust rose as thick as a cloud and acrid to the taste, the horses were fat and strong; they were running from the sheer love of it and would have raced past except for that far-spaced line of arm-waving men out there.

"It couldn't happen anywhere but here," Jane said quickly, lifted out of her silence by this scene.

Jeb looked around at her and back outward again.

"Once we had a feller workin' here from the east, an' he used to tell us what it's like back there. He said ten thousand acres was a sight o' land in the east. Seems unbelievable, don't it; ten thousand acres bein' a big spread back there?"

Jane turned, considered old Jeb a moment, then asked a question. "What part of the east was he from, Jeb; New York or perhaps New England somewhere?"

"No, ma'am. He was from Missouri. That's about

where Massachusetts is."

Jane's considering gaze turned solemn. "About there," she said softly, and turned back to watching all those horses funnel along into the corrals and begin running around and around in there.

Lex and old Hyatt gave orders, the *vaqueros* moved in to rope out team horses and saddle animals, the dust thickened, men's curses and chiding laughter rose through that dust, and the hour-long matter of selecting the correct animals for the cattle drive was under way.

Jeb pointed out a stocky, dark and villainous looking *vaquero* with a pock-marked face who seemed never to move. "That's Epifanio," he explained to Jane. "He's called Pifas for short. He's near as old as I am."

"No," breathed Jane, watching that sturdy, massive figure through layers of dun dust.

"Yes'm, he sure is. But you know, it's the peppers they eat keeps 'em young. How old's he look to you?"

"Thirty perhaps, Jeb. No more than thirty-five."

"Miss Jane, I can tell you he's got grandchildren down in Sonora."

They watched the one called Pifas. He had a large coil of rawhide rope in his left hand, a little sagging loop of the riata in his right hand. He stood there broadly smiling as horses flashed around him never once flinching as hooves and thousand-pound bodies came within inches of him. He was obviously enjoying this very much. Lex called out: "The blazed-faced sorrel with the roached mane, Pifas." That little fragile-seeming loop lifted, passed once backhanded around Pifas's head, sailed far out over a dozen plunging backs, settled neatly around a sorrel horse's neck and sang taut. The horse snorted, rolled both eyes and planted himself down stiff-legged. He was caught, the game was over, and one of the younger *vaqueros* moved in to lead this particular horse away.

Seventeen times that solidly massive and unmoving Mexican repeated this identical process, never missing a cast, never roping the wrong horse, and afterwards when the selection was completed, he casually coiled his riata, swaggered past the other cowboys still wearing that broad smile, and sauntered on out of the corral. His work was done; the lesser *vaqueros* took over from there.

"He's the *segundo*," explained Jeb. "Sort of straw-boss over the others. He's got a lot of pride, that one."

"He should have," said Jane. "I've never seen such dexterity and perfect timing before."

Jeb gravely nodded, watching Epifanio halt over by Lex and Hyatt Morgan. "That used to be my job," he said quietly, "a long time ago."

Ward came around the barn astride his sweaty horse, jumped down and flung his reins to Jeb. He had been told by his brother who was around here, waiting. His smile was a handsome combination of flashing white teeth and a smoothly sun-layered set of even features. He pushed back his hat, planted himself squarely before Jane and said, "If Lex hadn't told me I wouldn't have believed he'd ever allow it." Clearly,

Ward was referring to his father, and Jane took it that way.

She said, meeting his smile with a look of equal pleasure, "He rode into Tucson and asked me if I'd like to go along."

Ward swung, still expansively smiling. "Jeb, what do you think of that?" he loudly demanded.

Old Jeb looked skeptical and falsely pleased at the same time. "I think it's fine," he lied, and walked away with Ward's horse.

The cowboys came along leading several horses apiece. They were an earthy, simply band of men given to gaiety, to irresponsible good-nature in most things, and now as they moved along they laughed at one another, poked sly fun at peacock-proud old Epifanio walking along with them, and occasionally rolled liquid-dark eyes over where Jane stood. They were simple men with a fierce loyalty to their *patron,* but basically they were men; the sight of a beautiful girl stirred them as it also stirred the three Morgans.

Lex and old Hyatt came slowly striding on around from the corrals. They were quietly speaking back and forth, ceased this only when they sighted Ward and Jane standing in the barn's pleasant shade, then each in his own way reacted to the girl's presence. Old Hyatt said briskly, "Better give Jeb a hand with the wagon-hitch. Better ride on ahead with him too, and take Pifas with you; start the drive. We'll come along behind you—all the rest of us."

"*All* of you?" asked Lex quietly.

Hyatt looked around. "Yes. Her too. She can ride until she gets tired, then she can go along with Jeb in the wagon."

"It'll be back in the dusty drag by then," Lex reminded his father.

Old Hyatt nodded. "I know that," he said, and walked on over where his *vaqueros* were meticulously examining the hooves, the legs, the backs of their animals.

Lex watched his father moving off for a moment. He made a little crooked smile. He knew why Hyatt was doing this, so now he looked over where his brother and Jane were animatedly talking. She was, in Lex's astringent view, flawlessly beautiful. Somewhere, some time, he should have met her first. A man—every man—lives with a dream within him of his ideal woman. Perhaps though, this ideal was unattainable. At least that's what ran through Lex's mind now. Perhaps the reason he'd never found *his* ideal was because she didn't actually exist. She was, possibly, a composite with a face and figure as strikingly arresting as the face and figure of Jane Adair, yet with the same, softly-remembered depth of quiet strength his mother had possessed, and with the kind of laughter Lex imagined his ideal would have, along with her passion and her selflessness. It was, he concluded, asking a lot for all this to be inherent in one woman.

Old Jeb indignantly sang out, over where Epifanio was grinning at his efforts to harness a sleek-hided big raw colt. Lex's thoughts came back to the present; he started over to give Jeb a hand and as he strode past Ward and Jane he turned, saw the girl's steady grey gaze on him, and nodded in an expressionless, careful way.

Jeb was swollen with grim wrath at the skittish big colt by the time Lex came up. What made it worse was the old cowhand's inability to adequately express his vexation with Jane Adair within hearing, so he caught up a shot-loaded quirt and stepped up beside the fractious horse.

"Hold it," ordered big Lex, coming up. "Use that as the last resort, not the first," he stated, grabbed the big colt by its bit and when the beast refused to back along the wagon's pole to be hitched, Lex turned sideways, lifted his right foot and bore down with his spur rowel across the colt's coronet. The colt snorted with pain and flinched backwards. Lex rowelled him again. The colt backed away from him, two of the Mexicans caught his traces, hooked them and the fight was over. The second horse was led up harnessed, backed into place and also hooked up. He offered no resistance at all.

Jeb glowered at the big colt, gathered his lines and grunted up onto the box. "You comin' on with me?" he asked Lex, and got back a nod. "Good; 'cause I got a feelin' about this big dumbhead danged colt."

Lex crossed over where the *segundo* was grinningly holding his saddled mount, turned the horse once before mounting, for every one of these animals was green, and toed in to spring up. At that precise moment old Jeb flicked his lines. That orry-eyed big colt eased forward into his collar, felt the traces along his legs, snorted, rolled his eyes and gave a mighty forward lunge which nearly tipped old Jeb backwards off his seat. Jeb swore, the quiet horse moved ahead, and suddenly that big colt tried to run. He could not drag the tame horse and the laden wagon too, but he tried. Dust rose up as the wagon went bouncing on out of the yard westward, Jeb's blistering invective drifted back over the rumble and the rattle, and the six *vaqueros* doubled over with glee.

Lex settled down across his saddle, eased out his horse and started along after old Jeb's careening wagon. He too was smiling as he swung past his brother and Jane Adair.

Ward called out gleefully, "Let him go, Lex. He'll be five miles out before he quits cussin' long enough to kick the brake."

Lex did not respond to this. His gaze crossed the upward, somber look of Jane Adair, held for the little length of time it took for his horse to carry him on past, then the westward desert lay emptily ahead and on all sides as he booted his beast over into a loose lope in the wake of old Jeb's dust and faintly-heard howls of purest anger.

Those two eventually came together two miles out, where the herd was patiently grazing, scattered a little but not much, and where, as Ward had prophesied, old Jeb finally forgot enough of his indignation to set the rear-wheel brake and drag his wagon down to a halt.

Lex got down, walked over and considered the big green colt where he stood sweat-shiny and quaking in his harness. Jeb called the colt a name, slackened his lines and heaved a big sigh.

"Lex," he said, "what your paw done is pure bad luck."

For a moment big, taciturn Lex Morgan continued to study that green colt, acting as though he hadn't heard or didn't understand what old Jeb had said.

"Oh never mind that confounded horse," said Jeb, after a moment of silence. "I expected him to do something foolish." Jeb glared at the beast. "Lucky, as big and stout as he is, he didn't carry me along another couple miles." Jeb leaned far out to peer backwards where a spiraling cloud of dust showed that the others were coming on. He sat back and scowled at Lex where the younger man sauntered back to lean up a fore-wheel.

"I'm tellin' you, Lex, that's bad luck, bringin' a woman along on a drive like this. Your paw ought to know better too."

"Tell him, not me," said Lex, also gazing back where that churning dust stood straight upwards in the dry, clear air. "He's testing her, Jeb."

"Well, I know that, dammit all. I didn't come down in the last rain. I know why he's fetchin' her along, boy."

Lex swung his quiet gaze upwards. "Then you ought to also know that bellyachin' isn't going to change anything, Jeb. He invited her, she's here, and that's that."

"But it just ain't right, Lex. There'll be trouble if she's along sure as the devil."

"Trouble? What kind of trouble?"

"Well now I don't know that; if I did I'd know what to do about it, but females on cattle drives just naturally bring trouble. It's like a feller I met once in a Tucson saloon told me about takin' women on ships. He'd been a sailor an' he said it was bad luck to have women on board."

Lex's long, calm lips lifted slightly at their outer corners. He viewed old Jeb with a half-affectionate, half-indulgent expression. "We're not on a ship, this isn't the ocean, and if paw wants to test her grit maybe he's right. But . . ."

"Yeah? But what?"

Lex shrugged, turned, stepped up over leather and looked blankly down at the older man. "But I think he's wasting his time. She's got grit, Jeb, along with everything else a right handsome woman ought to have."

Lex spun his horse and rode out around the lead-team southward bound to pick up the drifting animals in that direction and start them along.

Old Jeb sat on his wagon seat watching Lex ride off. He seemed suddenly paralyzed by some blinding revelation. He ran a hand under his clean-shaven jaw, drew his eyes out narrow as he watched Lex lope southward, and after a while he let off a big, long audible sigh and said to his nigh-side horse, the quiet animal against which he had no rancor, "I'll be damned, Coaly. You know what just came to me? Lex's got some notion about that girl. I'll be double damned if I don't believe that's a danged fact."

From far back old Hyatt's long shout jerked Jeb straight up on his seat. He eased off the brake, put a cautious eye upon the sweaty colt and gently flicked the lines. The colt, contrary to Jeb's expectations, did not attempt to bolt again. He instead leaned in his collar as quietly as the tame horse also did, and the wagon started bouncing heavily along. It was laden with bedrolls, pans, pots, provisions, and the nearly endless impedimenta which invariably accompanied cattle drives such as extra ropes, branding irons, sacked flour and sugar, horse hobbles, even axes in this treeless land, and a square massive oaken box of extra ammunition.

FOUR

To strike Tanque Verde where some forgotten toilers had built a large, circular adobe water trough—or tanque—into which they had, with equally as herculean labors piped an underground spring to make a splash of trees and greenery—verde—in this vast desert emptiness, required nearly seven hours of steady riding for the *vaqueros,* and an uninterrupted shuffling-along of the great mass of rusty-red hided and wicked-horned Morgan cattle. What especially slowed the entire entourage was the drag, which was far back at the end of the drive where Jeb McCarty's wagon also was. Mostly, those drag-critters were swollen-up calvy cows. They would not hurry and in fact they physically could not. So, no one hurried them.

But the drag was a bitter place to be. There, all the settling dust came down thick enough to taste. Jeb had a bandana over his lower face. So also did the two *vaqueros* back there. They slouched along and sweated. For as long as daylight lasted it was very uncomfortable back there, but once mellow evening came, conditions improved. If the dust didn't atrophy then at least the heat lessened, and to men accustomed to hardship a mitigation of discomfort was as much as one dared hope for.

Jane Adair rode on the southerly wing of the herd with Ward. Far ahead at point position rode old Hyatt, one foot out of the stirrup so that he could, from time to time, twist and gaze backwards. On the north wing rode Lex and Epifanio Garcia, their postures slouched and bored. Along both sides of the drive rode the others, the Morgan Ranch *vaqueros*. Altogether, it was a routine drive, the land lay boring-empty, and when Tanque Verde showed up under a huge old yellow full moon, that same lethargic indifference still held all those people. There was no reason for it not to; with the exception of Jane Adair each of them had made this identical crossing many times over the years, they knew in advance what lay ahead and could, without seeming to be prophetic, say exactly what they would be doing ten hours hence, or ten minutes hence.

They remained back for a full hour, separated by distance but well within sight of each other, letting the cattle go ahead and tank up at the huge old adobe trough. Jeb used this time to go around, drop the tail-gate, set its chains in place and shake dust from a huge tin mixing pan. With the exception of old Hyatt, Jeb had made this trip more often than any of the others. He knew exactly what to do and when to start it, like now, as he began concocting a stew and later, when Hyatt halloed for them to come on up for camp. he stretched a cloth over the pan, made it fast underneath, went around and climbed back upon the seat to cluck his team ahead. He had a head-start on making supper now, exactly as he'd always figured to have during this lay-over time.

It was one of those nights Jane had spoken of to old Hyatt; utterly still, endlessly hushed and in some disturbingly indefinable way, sad.

The stars glowed without flickering respite. The moon hung up there scarcely seeming to move. From east to west the curvature of that vast purple overhead tapestry softly blanketed the Universe.

Pifas and one other *vaquero* made Jeb's little fire, provided faggots for future use, then went on over to the trough where the other Mexicans were idly smoking and talking, sometimes laughing, sometimes making those little derisively hooting calls at one another. It was a good, bland night, the kind that nurtured in every man whatever it was that lay uppermost in his heart and mind.

Hyatt strode over where Lex was washing, stripped to the waist. He approvingly considered the mighty chest, shoulders and upper arms of his elder son. He eased down upon the trough's worn-smooth edge and began to roll a brown-paper cigarette. He was a man at peace with himself and with his world. Moonlight tamed his rugged features, turned them soft-seeming in its pewter light. He lit up, snapped the match and dropped it. He rolled back his head and somberly gazed upwards.

Lex finished washing, dried off and shrugged back into his shirt but left his sweat-stained black hat there upon the trough's edge.

"Nice night," he said to his father. "Three years ago we got caught out here by one of those springtime flash-floods. You remember?"

"I remember. Have you seen your brother?"

Lex rolled his head sideways. "Walking out a way with Miss Jane."

"Yes," murmured old Hyatt, sounding as though he thought it should be this way between his youngest and the chosen mate of his youngest. "Well, maybe if that drag'll move along a little better, we can make it to Sonoita Canyon by this time tomorrow."

Lex shook his head in doubt about this. "Almost, maybe, but not quite. Be day after tomorrow in the morning when we hit Sonoita."

The old man didn't argue; he didn't really care. He

inhaled, exhaled and looked down at the little glowing tip of the cigarette in his hand. He shifted position slightly and looked out over the ghostly land, northward. Great mountains stood against the paler sky, their raw-edged peaks like daggers pointed at the underbelly of heaven. On full-moon nights particularly, he felt kinship with this land. He had come originally, many decades before, from the Staked Plains of Texas. He had come poor, with one old wagon and seven horses; with a lovely, willowy young wife and an emerging confidence in himself and his convictions.

It had been a long pull to get up where he now was. After the birth of young Ward it had also been a lonely pull with no one to share his dreams with, so, he had gradually become what he now was, a quiet man full of drive and relentlessness, but a fair and honest man, and yet that very fairness and honesty would some day be where the rub came, because the beliefs of old Hyatt Morgan were not the same beliefs of many others in this land. They were the convictions of an older breed of people, a pioneering caste; they were founded upon an unvoiced belief older perhaps than the race of such men as Hyatt Morgan. They said a man got an eye for an eye and a tooth for a tooth. They were the raw convictions of all pioneers who had ever pitted themselves against a hostile land. They had to be, for during old Hyatt Morgan's formative years, the man who showed pity or timidity, died young and went into the ground forgotten.

But on nights like this, with the musical lilt of liquid-soft Spanish sentences coming from around behind the wagon where the *vaqueros* loafed and smoked and talked with Jeb, and with that age-old big yellow moon up there, a man's softest instincts prevailed. For an hour or two on springtime full-moon nights a man might put aside everything of iron which was in him and become something entirely different.

"One time," said old Hyatt as Lex sat there beside him listening to the sound of running water behind them, "I came up here three hours ahead of a drive all alone, and there was a band of 'Pache bucks here restin' up after a run down into Mexico. I don't know who was most surprised, them or me." Old Hyatt dropped his smoke, stepped upon it and chuckled. "But I can sure tell you which one of us rode the hardest getting back where he came from."

Lex listened. He'd heard this story before but it still amused him because, ever since he could remember his father, he could not imagine old Hyatt running away from anything.

"Well," said the old man, standing up off the trough, "I can smell Jeb's stew. We'd better step along before the others clean us out." The old man threw up his head, looked around and very faintly scowled. "Maybe Ward can live on love but I don't think he ought to keep *her* out there too long. She's not used to ridin' this far in one day."

"Paw?"

Hyatt turned as Lex also got off the trough. They

were the same height and heft. "Yes."

"Don't stir Jeb up. He thinks it's bad luck havin' her along on the drive."

Hyatt inclined his head. "I know."

"You talked to him?"

"No, but after more'n twenty years I can read him like a book. When he went dusting it out of the yard with that spooky colt draggin' the whole she-bang along this afternoon, I could near him squawlin' up there on his wagon-seat. It was in his voice then, what was botherin' him. But don't worry, Lex, I'll give him all day tomorrow to cool down."

They started over towards the wagon side by side. There was a strong scent of sweaty animals in the still air, and along with it the equally as strong aroma of Jeb McCarty's cow-camp stew.

Epifanio came strolling along outward bound with his tin plate in one hand, his tin cup in the other. He flashed the Morgans a broad smile. White teeth shown in Epifanio's backgrounding dark and pock-marked face.

"Pifas," said the old man. "After supper why don't you take one of the others and scout around a little?"

Epifanio's smile suddenly winked out. *"Indios, Jefe?"* He softly asked, and made a sniffing motion with his wrinkled-up nose.

Hyatt laughed. "No Indians, Pifas. A man sometimes feels better when he beds down if he's plumb sure how things are around him in the night."

"Ahh," sighed the stocky, thickly powerful Mexican, obviously vastly relieved. "*Seguro, Jefe;* it shall be done." Pifas grinned and walked on.

Hyatt looked after him, wagged his head and started forward again. "Strange thing. No matter how brave they are at other times, if you want to scare a Mexican just mention there might be bronco Apaches around."

Lex made his own hollow little laugh. "Not just Mexicans," he told his father. "When Ward and I were little Jeb used to scare the devil out of us when we'd ride into the ranch after sundown with tales of what he'd seen the Indians do to captives."

They passed on around where the *vaqueros* were beginning to drift back out into the night with their suppers and old Jeb put a concerned and exasperated look upon Hyatt.

"Now where's that young idiot gone and walked that girl, anyway," he groused. "He knows how dangerous it can be walkin' out in the dark."

Lex turned and stood a long time looking out and around. His face too showed concern and yet it did not appear to be the same concern old Jeb was showing.

Hyatt went up, took his laden plate, one of the tin mugs with coffee in them and went back a little distance to drop down cross-legged beyond the fire. It was lifelong habit which kept him from sitting where he could be distinctly outlined by Jeb's cooking-fire. He said, "Get some supper, Lex, and quit worrying."

Lex started over to the tailgate too. Without a word Jeb filled a plate and passed it over. Then he turned on Hyatt with spirit, saying, "I reckon we all figured out why you brought her along."

Hyatt glanced up, chewed a long time in silence, dropped his eyes and went right on eating. He had no comment to make.

"Figured you were a better judge of folks than that," went on Jeb. Lex crossing over in front of him, went out where Hyatt was sitting and sank down. Jeb waited a moment then spoke again, directing his words to Hyatt as before. "She's got iron enough for the Morgans. Even I can tell that, an' I don't have to drag her all over kingdom come to prove it neither."

Hyatt put down his emptied plate, took up his coffee cup and gently swished it. He still said nothing. Where twisting firelight struck, it made his face look more hawk-like than ever. Reddish flames and old Hyatt's perpetually sun-darkened hide, plus a high-bridged nose and lean lips made it seem that Hyatt was an Indian sitting there. He looked at peace now, but with that peculiar underlying look of fierce temper latent in his expression such as many Indians possess.

Another man as old and seasoned as Jeb McCarty was, might have read that bronzed face differently and taken caution. Not Jeb. He went right on giving old Hyatt an indignant piece of his mind, and oddly, nothing happened. Hyatt sat there relaxed, listening, sipping his coffee and saying nothing. At his side even Lex looked over once or twice because his father's temper was notorious.

Finally, Jeb got it all off his chest, lapsed into silence and went about cleaning up the supper mess. Old

Hyatt got up, hitched at his shell-belt, sucked his teeth and detachedly watched Jeb muttering to himself as he worked. He stepped over, halted beside the other old man and softly said, "Pardner, it's been a long lifetime. I'm gettin' near the end of it. I can't afford any mistakes in the home-stretch. If what I'm doin' is obvious, I still got to do it, because it'll prove she's capable or she isn't. If she isn't, I got to know it now. So do you. Your stake in this is as big as mine. That boy belongs as much to you as to me."

Hyatt lifted a big, work-scarred hand, dropped it lightly upon Jeb's shoulder, let it lie there briefly, withdrew it and walked on out into the night where the bedrolls were.

Jeb stood completely still and silent until Hyatt was gone and even the soft, grinding sound of his bootfalls were also gone, then Jeb slumped, stood a moment gazing into his dishpan's oily water, took off his flour-sack apron to wipe his hands upon and turned around facing Lex. There was a hard wet shininess to the old *vaquero's* eyes which reflected starlight.

"I'm goin' to tell you somethin'," he said huskily, "and dang you, Lex Morgan, don't you never forget it. They only made one man like your paw. There'll never be another and in the past there ain't never been one before neither."

Old Jeb thunderously blew his nose and groped around for his tobacco sack, ducked his head and fiercely went to work making a smoke. He eventually lit up, exhaled and listened to the night. He had his back to Lex as the younger man rose up to put his dishes in the wash-pan and afterwards softly walk away.

FIVE

The camp became quiet, Jeb's little fire turned glowingly red, out where the cattle were bedded down one solitary night-hawk rode slowly around and around sometimes with the pinprick red glow of a cigarette showing, sometimes not. Hyatt lay with his head to the east, his feet to the west. Jeb snored with oblivious abandon and somewhere over by the trough a drinking horse made his chuckering little sounds.

Lex lay there cataloguing all the night-sounds: one of the *vaqueros* softly babbled in his sleep near the trough and another one, a lighter sleeper evidently, hissed for that sleeper to wake up and shut up. The babbler went on with his soft Spanish patter, the annoyed man dropped back down, and the night ran on.

Overhead a million little tears glistened in the firmament. That enormous old yellow moon went on its serene left-to-right crossing and a long distance off a desert wolf raised his head and let off wild and lonely calls.

Lex heard all these things, placed each in its correct category, raised up once to look over where his brother's untouched bedroll was, and felt a knife turning slowly in his vitals.

That old wolf tongued again, closer this time, and

suddenly Hyatt raised up fifty feet off with the soft light lying across his face. Lex watched.

Hyatt was completely still over there for a long time. He seemed not to notice anything around him. The third time that wolf tongued he swung back his blankets with one practiced movement and rolled out, tugged on his boots, scooped up his shell-belt, his hat, and glided across to where old Jeb was snoring. Lex saw him drop to one knee beside the wagon, place a hand lightly upon Jeb's chest and at once that snoring choked off.

But old Jeb neither sprang up at that touch nor even moved, as far as Lex could make out. Those two briefly whispered back and forth, Jeb reared up, and the pair of them, dark-blending there beside the wagon, remained as still as stone for a long while. Lex felt hair rise up at the base of his skull. Something swished in the trampled grass at his side and he nearly sprang out of his blankets. It was Epifanio Garcia, his dark face spring-tight and smooth with inner dread. He put his head down close to whisper.

"Indios!"

All the ancient Mexican terror reverberated in that one word. Lex looked around where Epifanio knelt with both hands locked around a Winchester carbine.

"The wolf?" he asked.

"*Si.* Yes; it is the wolf who is not a wolf. I'll tell your father; you get on your gun and your boots."

"Wait. My father already knows. He's over with Jeb at the wagon."

Epifanio looked across into the night with straining eyes, his ragged breathing audible, his crouch stiffly unnatural and attuned to instant reaction. At the slightest sound beyond camp he would whip upright, perhaps start shooting.

Lex rolled out, stamped into his boots, buckled on his shell-belt, lashed down the holster and picked up his carbine. To Epifanio he said softly, "Go waken the men. Bring them to the wagon. Not a sound, Pifas; remember that." He then slipped over where his father and old Jeb were. Those two rolled solemn looks over at him and said nothing. He joined them at their listening.

The wolf tongued once more.

"Closer," whispered Jeb, feeling around for his boots and gun.

Lex suddenly moved away from them. He peered inside the wagon where Jane Adair's bed had been made. It was empty. He paced silently across where Ward's bedroll still lay where it had been flung down, still rolled and tied at both ends. He sank to one knee over there feeling suddenly sick to his stomach. Behind him the *vaqueros* went gliding past towards the wagon. One of them had neglected to remove his huge Chihuahua spurs and Epifanio turned to fiercely hiss at this one. The Mexican dropped down at once and shucked those softly musical big-rowelled appendages, then he jumped up and fled along after his *compañeros,* unwilling even in the heart of their camp to be alone.

Lex got heavily back upright plumbing the onward night for some hint of what lay out there where his brother and Jane Adair had been so silently swallowed up. Hyatt came soundlessly over and gazed down at that untouched bedroll, grounded his carbine and leaned upon it keeping his face averted. Even the strongest of men are weak where the heart is concerned.

"We can wait," Lex said softly, "or we can go out there and get in the first licks."

Hyatt rallied; his profile was its usual iron self again but there was an echo of tragedy in his husky voice. "Jeb's already slipped out with Raul Hernandez. We'll wait." Hyatt broke off, spent a moment looking out into the ghostly gloom, then he lifted his carbine, saying, "Come on; we should be over at the wagon."

They went over where Epifanio and the five remaining *vaqueros* huddled in strained silence, joined that wide-awake, apprehensive vigil and felt each second pass with its little dragging feet.

The wolf did not howl again, but a swift-fox yapped, making that agitated little nervous half-bark, half-snarl swift-foxes made. "Hernandez," breathed Epifanio, but so thoroughly realistic had that sound been that Lex was not at all sure Pifas was correct.

"It could fool an Apache," murmured Lex, doubtfully.

"It's the hardest of all sounds to simulate," said his father. "But remember, son, Raul was raised an Apache."

But none of them were certain, including Epifanio Garcia, who only hoped the *vaquero* Hernandez had made that call; hoped it with all his heart, for like many brave Mexicans, Epifanio would fight a lion in broad daylight, but in the night with all the chilling tales of boyhood to rise up and become vivid in his imagination, the smell or sight or even the suggestion of Apaches, turned him into much less of a man than he normally was.

But it was Hernandez; he and old Jeb came slipping back without a sound, a pair of faint-seen shadows edging around the wagon to come up behind those huddled watchers and breathe a very faint warning in breathless Spanish.

Raul Hernandez, kidnapped as a baby and raised as an Apache for fifteen of his twenty-three years, was a lithe, panther-like *vaquero,* quick as a cat and seemingly younger than his age with a boyish, candid face and black eyes that missed nothing. He sank down to one knee with Jeb at his side, lifted his left arm and rigidly pointed north-westward. In the uniquely guttural, throaty Spanish of Mexicans raised as Apaches, he said, "No Indians—these are the riders of other people's horses from Sonora. *Mala hombres*—bad men. They have *esillas vaqueros*—cowboy saddles from Mexico. No Indian rides *esillas vaqueros.* And they have *sombreros vaqueros;* Indians do not wear hats of Mexican cowboys."

"Renegade raiders," put in Jeb softly. "We got up an' skylined 'em."

"How many?" Hyatt asked.

Jeb did as a Mexican might have done; he lifted his shoulders and let them fall. "*Quien sabe?* Who knows? Where we first spotted them it looked like a pretty big band, Hyatt."

"Ten, twenty, thirty—fifty?"

"Twelve maybe or fifteen. A lot more guns than we have."

Lex said, "Never mind the guns or the numbers; did you find anything else out there?"

They knew what he meant and all of them gravely turned to await the answer. Hernandez shook his head. "We saw nothing, but I think maybe your brother and the woman are there, because they were all looking back where several of them were dismounted and arguing."

"You heard them argue?"

"*Si,* we could hear anger in some voices but it was too distant to make out the words." Hernandez turned towards Jeb as though for confirmation of this. Jeb nodded, then pointed northward.

"There's a chance, if we move out quickly, we might get around behind them before they make a run on the herd and stampede it." Jeb looked squarely at old Hyatt. "It'll be the cattle and horses they want. Ward and Miss Jane—well—I'd say they was sneakin' up on us, found them out strollin' in the dark, and they were just a sort of bonus."

"To hell with the herd," growled old Hyatt, but Lex cut across this with quick, hard words.

"Raul; Pifas; go out and bring in our horses." Epifanio rolled his eyes and opened his mouth at this order, so Lex said, "All right; all six of you go catch our horses. If they get organized enough to make a run on the herd we can't let 'em set us afoot. Go on—and no noise. Above all else—no noise!"

The *vaqueros* stood up stiffly, peered around and started silently away in the direction of the big adobe trough. "Scairt stiff," mumbled Jeb, "all but that Hernandez. I never been out with him before. He can out-Indian any 'Pache I ever saw. He's part wolf an' part snake."

Hyatt sighed, raised his eyes to the others and quietly said, "I can thank God. Apaches would have gone to work on them immediately; staked them out, stuffed their mouths with grass and—"

"Shut up," snarled Lex, and so upset were all three of them that they didn't even notice that this was the first time Lex had ever spoken like that to his father. "They aren't Apaches, they're Mex guerillas, so they'll take Ward and Jane with them. Paw, if they stampede the cattle we cannot shoot."

Hyatt nodded. So did old Jeb.

"If we have the time, paw, let's try and talk to them. Try and ransom Ward and Jane."

Hyatt's head whipped up. His eyes suddenly burned with new hope. But almost as quickly as that hope was born it died. Out in the northward night a wolf howled. Further west and slightly southward, an answering call sounded. It was too late, the renegades were beginning their maneuver, they were easing down as close as they could to the Morgan herd, some off in the sooty west to prevent the animals from breaking away in the wrong direction, some from northward and probably eastward, preventing the stampede from swinging in those directions.

"Straight south towards the border," muttered old Jeb, correctly gauging those signals, correctly placing the unseen marauders by their simulated animal calls. "If we do nothing they'll think they've caught us plumb asleep."

Lex stood up, cocked his head then turned westerly. Somewhere out there horses could be faintly heard walking along. Hyatt and Jeb also heard and stood up. Moments later the *vaqueros* came stepping along with long, thrusting strides. They too had heard, and correctly interpreted, those signal-calls, and now as they came up leading the saddle animals, their eyes were round and glassy with apprehension.

"Ropes," snapped old Hyatt. "Put long ropes on your mounts, boys. When they hit that herd they'll come shootin'. You can't hold a horse with a little catch-rope when he's panicked by gunfire. Get your ropes on 'em and quickly!"

They were hastening to obey when somewhere northward a man's shrill scream rang out. Instantly the sound of wildly racing horses broke the stillness. There were other shouts now too, as renegade raiders from Mexico swept down upon the bedded Morgan herd.

Epifanio, with his snorting horse standing close,

lifted a carbine. Lex struck it aside. "No firing. No firing any of you."

"*Señor*—what of the herd?"

"Let 'em have it gawddamn it, that girl and my brother are out there. The hell with the cattle."

Epifanio subsided. The other *vaqueros,* with excited horses to keep an eye upon, also put aside their carbines. For a short while there was just that drum-roll thunder of riders, then gunshots erupted, red flashes lashed skyward as the renegades hit the herd, cattle sprang up in panic, swung southward trampling each other, bawling in purest fright, and the earth shook underfoot with the abrupt eruption of a wild-flinging rush as seven hundred animals ran blindly along ahead of those recklessly-riding marauders.

One man, coming in from the east, swerved at sight of Jeb's wagon canvas in the moonlight. This raider seemed to wish for one or two good clean shots at the *norteamericanos,* for he held his .45 balanced upright as he raced along peering earthward where the empty bedrolls lay. They all saw this one; he came within a hundred feet of the wagon. Hyatt stepped out in front, his right hand swooping downward and upward in a blur of practiced movement. He cried out.

"*Vaquero!*"

The raider twisted in the saddle whipping downward with that cocked .45. Hyatt fired, drew back his hammer, held the trigger fully back and lifted his thumb. The hammer dropped solidly down a second time, mushrooming crimson muzzleblast struck blindingly outward and upward and the Mexican's body wrenched suddenly upright. The horseman's gun exploded, his horse shied violently as that bullet burned its shoulder, and the raider made a wild grab for a handful of mane hair. He missed and fell.

Raul Hernandez sprang ahead past Lex, past old Hyatt, got almost to the fallen marauder when the man rolled over and sat up. He saw Raul coming, saw the watery flash of an upraised dagger and tried frantically to roll clear. He didn't make it. Raul dropped upon him. His knife-hand rose and fell, rose and fell.

"Enough," cried out Epifanio. "Enough, Raul. You have his life; do you want his soul too?"

But the killing of that solitary raider was almost lost in the violent thunder of all those stampeding hooves, the keening screams and the flashing tongues of many guns. For a long while those men by the Morgan wagon stood with their nervous horses, listening, peering southward where that careening herd was plunging along, making their private calculations on the direction, the probable number of men involved, and how all this had so suddenly happened.

One hour ago most of them were blissfully sleeping. Two hours ago they were laughing beneath a benign old yellow moon.

SIX

They went forward to halt around Raul Hernandez, who had put up his knife, and gaze at the dead marauder. The man's chest was criss-crossed with the bullet-filled bandoleers of Mexican irregulars. He wore two tied-down six-guns and the tight-fitting gaudily embroidered *pantalones*—trousers—of Northern Mexico.

Hyatt toed the man over so that moonlight fell across his face. It was a brutal, coarse face and even in death the man showed that cruel imperviousness which was common among his kind.

"No good," muttered Epifanio, and called the dead man a name.

Hyatt turned away, saying, "Saddle up. Jeb, hand out extra ammunition. Travel light, men. One canteen and a pocketful of jerky. Nothing more." He looked from Epifanio to Lex, then half-turned and brushed Raul Hernandez's arm with his fingers. "You know the secret trails southward from here, don't you; the raider trails?"

"*Si, Jefe,*" replied the lithe *vaquero,* his black eyes still smoky from killing. "I know them."

"You lead out then. And Raul—not too far ahead. You understand?"

Hernandez inclined his head. He and Hyatt Morgan understood one another: Apache custom was for strong-heart bucks to slip away on their own and count a coup—sneak up on an enemy and silently knife or strangle him, then return with the dead man's wallet, his watch, his guns, to show his great prowess. Raul Hernandez, raised as an Apache, would have the same bronco-buck desires: Hyatt understood, but would not have his son or Jane Adair jeopardized. That's what he'd meant when he warned Hernandez not to get too far ahead.

They went back to the wagon with the night once more emptily hushed and deceptively benign. They rigged out, stuffed pockets with shells from the broken-open box Jeb left on the tailgate, got astride and filed off southward behind Raul Hernandez.

Hyatt rode with Lex on one side, old Jeb on the other side. None of them spoke. Further back, also riding closed-up, was Epifanio Garcia and the others, every one of them very conscious of the cordite stench in the air, along with the tangy smell of cattle.

The Santa Cruz River lay somewhere off on their left. On their right, dimly discernible as ghostly outlines, stood the broken ramparts of the Sierrita Mountains. These sprawling ramparts were strung out north and south with a slight bulge to the west which was not noticeable in the soft night.

They lost the sound of the Morgan cattle almost at once, but Hyatt would permit no haste. "We'll get them," he kept saying whenever one of the others would urge speed. "They can't go fast driving that large a herd of cattle."

Lex though was impatient. By the time they came even with the ghostly silhouette of ancient Mission San Xavier Del Bac, off on their right and gloomily dark in the night, he told his father he would take Raul Hernandez and push on ahead.

"You'll stay with the rest of us," exclaimed old

Hyatt flintily. “We’re not going to do a damned thing that might endanger your brother or Miss Jane.”

So they persevered, kept riding southward down the moon-drenched night speaking a little now and then, until they crossed a meandering burro trail, and here Hernandez got down, left his horse with Epifanio, and trotted off to study tracks.

The others had a smoke, all but old Hyatt who sat his saddle as grim-faced and iron-like as he’d ever been. Lex dismounted, checked his cinchas, his horse’s legs, even his weapons. All these were impatient gestures; outlets for a frustrated energy and old Jeb read them as such when he sauntered over, blew out smoke and said quietly, “Your paw’s right, Lex. Slow and careful is the best way. They can’t make it back over the line with those cattle before tomorrow, and they’ll hole up somewhere. Then we’ll find ’em.”

Raul returned and reported. With quick, sharp gestures he thrust an upflung arm southward. “They’ve kept the herd going straight towards Mexico.” He then shifted that rigid arm to the right, or slightly westward. “But six of them broke off here and took this little road.” Raul dropped his arm, narrowed his black eyes and thoughtfully said, “I think they are wise. There are many horse-tracks along this little road. They think to fool us by separating like that; they believe we will follow the cattle while six of them get away in this fashion.”

Hyatt nodded gravely and softly said, “Which way would they take the prisoners?”

With no hesitation Raul said, "Westward, *Jefe.* Why else would they split up? Some of them wish only to get the herd in Mexico and sell it. Some of them are more interested in the beautiful *gringa* and your son, the one for what purposes you can imagine, the other for ransom."

Raul looked upwards and shrugged. He had said exactly what he believed, any decisions which must be made were no concern of his.

Hyatt twisted, looked back at the watching, listening men, and barked an order. "Mount up. We go west. Damn the herd."

Raul Hernandez led off again. He would, from time to time, lope ahead, dismount, bend far over and shuffle along like that for a short distance before remounting and waiting beside the little meandering roadway for the others to come up. Then they would all wordlessly ride along again.

There was a faint rind of soft light widening over along the eastern skyline by the time their little woodcutter's road led them through a pass between two nipple-like peaks called locally Twin Buttes. After that their little road kept getting fainter and fainter as those who over the years had made it, had branched off here and there making for their favorite woodcutting sites.

Now the going became slower and Hyatt began to show the strain. Once he said to old Jeb: "It'll be daylight directly. They'll be watching their back-trail sure. We've got to hole-up, but I want to be closer if it's possible."

Raul, as though he'd read Hyatt's mind, suddenly booted his horse over into a lope and flagged for the others to hasten along after him. It was light enough now for him to read the fresh sign without dismounting as he'd been compelled to do before, when visibility was poorer.

They loped for a mile, put Twin Buttes squarely behind them, and came out in the big, long valley lying between the easternmost Sierritas and the more westerly peaks of the same mountains.

This was a broad, long expanse of eerie emptiness, as silent and ghostly as another world. They stopped twice to listen, but heard nothing either time and resumed their way. Hyatt's impatience, under the old man's iron control, was fiercely demanding, and although he never once urged Hernandez to do better, it was clear that this slow-going was purest agony to him.

Lex was riding with Jeb now, directly behind his father and Raul Hernandez. From the corner of his eye Lex sighted a momentary flash of tiny light far off on their left. He threw up a hand to halt the cavalcade.

"Watch down southward there," he said. "Someone just lit a smoke down there."

They sat for a long time as still as statues, but there was no second match-flare. Jeb said impatiently to Raul Hernandez, "Does it look like they might've gone down there from the tracks?"

Raul shook his head. "No, *Señor.* So far the tracks lead straight ahead." Raul straightened in the saddle as a sudden notion came to him. "But we can be sure, I think. You all go southward and I will ride down the westward tracks. If my tracks curve southward I will find you; if they do not, you will hear a swift-fox cry out."

Hyatt nodded agreement with this, shortened his reins and swung off southward in a loose lope. The others hurried along behind him. Somewhere back in the night Raul Hernandez faded out in this lightless long valley between two sets of high peaks where that pre-dawn soft light could not reach.

Lex slowed his father with a low warning. "It wasn't too far ahead: we'd better slow down or they'll hear us coming."

Jeb and the others hauled back but Hyatt loped onward another hundred feet before slowing. This, though, was his only outward display of anxiety.

They were now closer to the westerly peaks than to the ones behind them, and here the run-off water had for centuries sluiced along at the base of the mountains making a huge north-south wash of almost cavernous dimensions. There was room in that forty-foot deep place for five herds of cattle as large as the stolen Morgan herd. On the desert side that huge basin had a gentle inward and downward slope, but far across, against the bony flanks of those barren granite slopes, the under-cut had been less gentle. Over there only in a very few places could a horse climb upwards, and even in those rare places where shale-slides made this at least feasible, the granite hillsides above offered no footing whatsoever for animals or men.

Every man in the Morgan crew had at one time or another been to this wash before, either hunting strayed cattle or running wild horses, which were common here, so it was natural that they all viewed the wash with sudden interest.

Hyatt had said the marauders would have to hole-up soon, before daylight, and this canyon-like big erosion gully was ideal for their purpose. But as Lex said to Jeb McCarty, if the raiders meant to hide the stolen herd in the Brawley Wash, why hadn't they brought the herd westward where their companions had split off from them?

Before Jeb could suggest a reason, old Hyatt drew rein, turned and answered for him. "If they keep the herd traveling southward to within a few miles of the border, they can swing westward down at Cerro Colorado—Red Mountain—cut through and still put the herd in Brawley Wash. It doesn't end until it's that far south of here."

Jeb screwed up his face to make some mileage calculations. He then dubiously waggled his head back and forth. "That's another five miles at least," he said. "Maybe more. It'll be daylight in another hour, Hyatt. Unless they run all the glue off them cattle every inch of the way, they can't possibly cover that much ground."

"What do they care about the tallow on those critters?" barked Hyatt. "All they want is to get 'em over the line alive. Starving peons in Sonora Province'll eat anything that can walk. You know that, Jeb."

"Jefe," whispered Epifanio Garcia, and raised one hand for silence. They all turned, peering back the way they had come. There was a rider approaching in a long lope.

"Chihuahua!" said Epifanio, making his broad smile and looking enormously relieved. "It is Raul."

Jeb grunted; his temper was wearing thin; men of his age, or the age of old Hyatt Morgan, needed rest, without it they became prickly with annoyance at the slightest disturbance.

"Who'd you figure it was," he growled at Epifanio, "Geronimo?"

"Amigo," answered Garcia softly, "in this place one never knows until—pssssft!—there is an arrow in one's soft parts."

"Oh hell," grumbled old Jeb, and might have said more but Raul Hernandez came riding up and threw a casual nod at Lex.

"You were right; they are down here somewhere. The tracks cut southward near the wash and went along it."

Raul eased his weight over slightly to one side in the saddle, looked slit-eyed down the southward flow of ghostly, hushed land, sniffed at the cool air and pursed his lips. He was coming to some kind of a decision. Even old Hyatt did not urge him in this. Finally he said, "I think they have two plans in mind. One is to hope we follow the cattle tracks southward until they are perhaps lost in the desert—which we have not done. The other is to take their *prisoneros* to some secret place, wait out the daylight, then meet again southward after nightfall again, and all join together in getting the herd down into Mexico."

"All right," said Hyatt roughly. "You know these mountains; where would they hide the prisoners?"

Raul shrugged. "Knowing the mountains is one thing," he murmured. "Knowing which of the many places they might hide their captives is another."

Hyatt regarded the lithe *vaquero* in strong silence then he said, "Track 'em, Raul. Somewhere down here they'll make a turn to hide in the wash or cross over into the westward hills. When you get to that spot stop. We'll scout on foot after that." Hyatt squared up in the saddle. "We'll find them. Now let's get moving."

Raul rode ahead again, cut briefly back and forth until he picked up fresh shod-horse marks, and went steadily along following this sign. Upon the east slopes of the mountains on their right, pink brightness appeared up near the peaks, then slowly and inexorably began its descending march down towards the gloomy valley where those men rode along. Lex particularly watched the progress of that revealing soft brightness; if they were still out here when dawn finally came, those fleeing marauders would surely catch sight of them, for no man fled for his life without keeping a sharp watch on his back-trail.

But Raul suddenly halted, let the others come up, and wordlessly pointed out where the shod-horse tracks went abruptly westward down into the wide wash, on across, and although they could not see that far, they knew those tracks also emerged from the wash over where a rare little sloping sidehill lay, covered with cured grass. Beyond that place lay a faintly discernible break in the barren slopes. There was undoubtedly a pass over there, which meant there was also a trail over there.

Hyatt pushed his horse on down into the wash and straight across it. Their conjectures proved correct, there was a way up out of the wash and they took it, riding one behind the other. Then they were in a world of heat-warped, inhospitable and razor-sharp jagged rock.

SEVEN

They left the horses where Raul Hernandez, his head tilted to sniff the air, said, "Dust. They are not too far ahead now."

Hyatt got stiffly down, wrenched out his Winchester and looked around at the others to say, "Fetch the water along. When that sun gets up we're going to need it."

From this point on Hyatt led them. He was good at this quiet stalking. With his carbine held loosely in both hands up across his body the old cowman pushed along the gritty trail which angled along through here, deeper into the tomb-like mountains.

There was not a tree, a bush, and only very rarely

even any little tufts of grass here. This was a lost world left over from the dawn of history; a place where horned-toads and lizards, rattlesnakes and a few strange birds lived. Further south the Sierritas became green and lush, with trees, and even a sky-blue little lake, but where Hyatt led them stealthily along now, there was nothing to show that life could exist here. And yet this was an ideal place for the Mexican marauders to hide with their captives for anyone sitting atop one of the overhead ramparts could see for fifty miles in any direction. Unless pursuers had, as the Morgan men had been able to do in the night, got underneath those rocky escarpments ahead of daylight, they could not possibly sneak up on anyone in these hills. That was why, Raul Hernandez confided in old Jeb and young Lex, the Apaches had favored these particular hills in preference to the further-south slopes where there was grass and shade.

Hyatt called a rest-halt a few moments before the sun jumped out over the westerly mountains. It was still cool but the close air of that confined little canyon they were passing through had an odd smell of metallic rock-heat in it. By high noon this narrow, breathless place would be insufferable.

Several of the *vaqueros* were put to keeping watch overhead. It was still gloomy in the canyon but that would not last, now that the sun was up, and this worried Hyatt. If visibility improved while they were still down in this place, and if the raiders were up above looking down, the Morgan men could be wiped out in the canyon. There was no place at all to hide from overhead gunmen.

Lex drank sparingly, watched his father cross over and sink down next to Raul Hernandez and speak quietly. Raul listened and replied. He also made arm-gestures which were eloquent to the others, including Lex; Hernandez knew this place and was explaining to old Hyatt how it lay, how all this land lay.

Jeb leaned over, dropped his voice and said, "Lex, we sit around in here much longer and it'll be light."

"Don't under-estimate Hernandez," said the younger man. "He's more Apache than Mex."

"Humph!" grunted old Jeb. "Lots we don't know about that young feller, but I can tell you this much—if he hasn't been riding these trails with 'Pache reavers before, then I'm a monkey's uncle."

Epifanio came over, grunted down, wiped sweat off his villainous face and smiled at the other two. Lex looked around, saying, "Pifas, what about Hernandez?"

Epifanio spread his hands. "I told you the story. He was taken as a small boy by *Indios*. They raised him. He ran away and wandered into a mission school. That's where he learned to rope and to know cattle. That's where I hired him and brought him to the ranch for the *patron's* approval. He is a fine horseman and good with a riata too."

"Yeah," muttered old Jeb, "and right handy with that boot-knife he carries too."

"Well," said Epifanio quietly, "what would you do,

viejo; have him go over to that raider back at our camp and offer him the hand of comradeship, when those men stole our cattle and our people?"

Jeb didn't answer. Hyatt and Raul Hernandez got up and motioned for the others to do the same, then the old cowman and the lithe Mexican started on up the canyon with the others following along once more.

From here on the land lifted, the trail they were following began to show little patches of soil and grass, and down from some high place a steady cool breeze blew against the climbers.

Behind them the world was soft pink and beginning to turn the faded, hot lemon color of full daytime, but in their canyon, night shadows lingered, which was helpful, for although they could tell by that fresh little breeze they were nearing the canyon's ending, they still were not safely clear of its lethal narrowness yet.

Hyatt strode along up ahead with Raul Hernandez, and once Hyatt halted as Raul spoke briefly to him and glided on ahead where a switch-back in the trail left no chance to see on around.

Raul returned, shrugged, and the whole party resumed its way. Now that breeze was fresher still, and cooler, as though it were coming down from some uncluttered open place. Jeb said, "It won't be long now," and wrinkled his nose at the clean fragrance of that little breeze.

Jeb was right. They came to a broad place in the trail beyond which the land abruptly brightened with sunlight and showed catclaw bushes, nopal, and even several spidery, graceful paloverde trees. Here, Hyatt and Raul left them and scouted on ahead. The *vaqueros,* still watching every overhead break and jagged spire, were uncomfortable. Epifanio hissed a forced kind of joviality to them, but it didn't help; they dreaded Apaches and regardless of what Hyatt or Lex or even Raul Hernandez had said, this was still Apache country.

Lex, watching the way they gripped their guns and sweated, said to Jeb he thought their men would be relieved to meet Mexican raiders up in this tumbled place of tilted slopes and up-ended huge rocks. Jeb's comments about the courage of the *vaqueros* was something less than flattering.

"In a place like this," he said, "give me Texans."

Hyatt and Raul came soft-footing it back, drew the men around them and old Hyatt, with his eyes nearly hidden behind the droop of lids, said briskly, "There are six horses about a half-mile ahead in a little pot-hole where there's grass and a hollowed-out catch-basin full of water. Looks like an old Indian hide-out; Raul says it is. Those are the marauders' animals, boys, and we're goin' to make cussed sure we get between 'em and their horses."

Lex said: "All right; but where are the people?"

Raul made a little fluttery gesture with his hands. "There are some old caves up ahead. They could be in any of them. Also, there are some overhead places where men can find shade. *Quien sabe?* Who knows where they are? I only think they will not be far from their horses, and that somewhere close around here, they will have a man sitting atop a rock watching."

Hyatt pointed a finger at Lex and Jeb. "You two go find that sentinel. We got to eliminate him before we dare go on ahead across the open country towards those horses. Where we're standin' right now is the last place there's any cover. From here on, if they're watchin', they can spot movement easy. So . . ."

"Yeah," said Lex. "Come on, Jeb."

"Careful," warned old Hyatt. "Before you take a chance remember that two lives depend on you. If those men think they're cornered they'll kill the hostages."

Lex handed Epifanio his carbine. Jeb also shed his Winchester. Aside from the fact that from here on what they had to do would be close work, those rifles would reflect sunlight. Raul stepped over and smilingly offered Lex his dagger. Lex shook his head and walked off.

Around the bend where that open place lay, and beyond it where those green-trunked paloverdes stood, was a pitilessly revealing splash of fresh sunlight. Jeb noticed this and profanely growled under his breath. He was no novice at this business of stealth and stalking, but he took no pleasure in doing it under a dazzling sun.

Lex though, swung down below the open place, wound his way around it by keeping to a buck-run which was less than eight inches wide, and in this fashion kept them both from being visible to any overhead watcher. But this was a dangerous undertaking; one mis-step on the left would send either one of them or both of them plunging straight down for two hundred feet into a narrow, lava-rock canyon and death. Old Jeb's shirt turned sodden before he'd half-traversed that buck-run, and when they eventually got back onto solid ground beyond the paloverdes and he could look back, he wanly shook his head.

On their right, around a thick shoulder of barren granite, and lower down, was that hidden little green place where six horses lazily grazed. Lex turned, made a careful study of the visible lifts and rises, then dropped his head, satisfied they were not under surveillance, and said, "Jeb, something here bothers me. There are six horses down there. Does that mean Ward and Jane and four raiders are around here somewhere, or does it mean there are six raiders, and Ward and Jane. Did they bring 'em here ridin' double, or did they bring 'em here on extra horses?"

"Extra horses," said Jeb at once. "Mex marauders almost always, when they make a ride deep into Arizona, fetch along a few extra mounts." Jeb also cocked a skeptical gaze around and back again. "We're up against four raiders, not six. I'll stake money on that."

"Yeah," said Lex dryly, "you might as well stake your money, Jeb. You're already stakin' your life."

They smiled at one another, eased around to study those horses for a long while, then drew back to compare deductions.

"The saddles are probably underneath this ledge we're standin' on; that's why we can't see 'em," opined Jeb. "Which probably means they came up here the same way we did. Now then, did you see that faint moccasin-trail on over the little meadow about halfway, leadin' westward up higher into the overhead rocks?"

Lex nodded and said, "That'll be the way they walked to where they are now."

"Right," pronounced Jeb. "All we got to do is find that damned sentry, and from where he'll be squattin' we'll be able to see the others."

Lex swung his head to shake off sweat. He dryly smiled at old Jeb beside him. "You sure make it sound simple," he said. Old Jeb grinned back.

"As far as I know," he said, "aren't any of us on this earth indefinitely, an' while I sure got no cravin' to die in a god-forsaken place like this, let's get movin'."

They went back, hugging their vertical shoulder of granite, felt its heat beginning to pile up around them, came to a definite break and halted long enough for Lex to get belly-down and poke his bare head on around for a long look.

Lex remained prone for so long old Jeb began to get fidgety. They were entirely exposed to the south; besides that, it was getting hotter by the minute. Then Lex sucked back, got up, struck rock-dust off his clothing and jerked a thumb over one shoulder.

"Well, Jeb," he laconically said, "we've found him."

"Huh? You saw him?"

"Get down and have a look. Watch to the north up along that saw-toothed rim on your right, and slightly ahead to the west. He's sitting up there with his legs danglin' down and he's got a big Mex sombrero on, plain as day."

Jeb stepped around, dropped flat, doffed his hat and craned for a look. He too remained prone for a long time before drawing back, and meanwhile Lex studied ways of crossing this little open place. There was a way to do it without that sentinel sighting them, but it would be as perilous as crossing the buck-run had been. When Jeb finally eased back Lex traced out the way they had to go.

"Over the edge," he explained, "and around underneath this place where we're sittin' now, then up onto solid ground again where the rock-shoulder begins again."

"Consarn it," grumbled old Jeb, "I wish your paw'd sent Pifas or Raul up here with you. Those drop-offs gives me the creeps."

"You just said none of us are here indefinitely, Jeb."

"Yeah," growled the old cowboy, "but I didn't say I was in any big rush to depart, neither."

They didn't find any game trail this time, and to make things worse, while there was a slope below the flat, it was in places sheer and blown clean of earth-covering by the winds which in winter-time scourged this bleak land. Lex got down over the edge first, tested the footing, found it amply solid, and turned to watch old Jeb also ease over the raw edge.

"Stay in my footsteps," he counseled the older man.

They began their dangerous work. It was impossible to move ahead more than a foot at a time. The distance to be traversed was no more than a hundred feet, but it took them a half-hour to do it, and by the time Lex got across, Jeb was wilted with anguish. Afterwards, lying together in pitiless sunlight, the older man made a big, rattling sigh, looked back, and said, "Did I ever tell you, boy, that I'm scairt to death of high places?"

Lex patted Jeb on the shoulder, got up and without bothering to dust himself off, stepped ahead to the protection of that continuing shoulder of hot stone again. He could, by standing quietly and studying the onward lay of land, discern a way of achieving that same saw-toothed rim where the raider-sentinel sat. He gestured to Jeb and started on.

Now, although there were still drop-offs on their right, they were in no danger from that quarter, for they had an upward climb along a bony side-hill which was no less than a hundred feet wide, and after that, where the side-hill flattened and the rim-rocks began, it was still fifty feet wide.

They halted once in a cluster of the broken, up-ended boulders of that ridge, to catch their breath and lie prone studying the man sitting a thousand yards dead ahead.

"Good going all the way," said Lex. "Plenty of boulders to hide behind."

Jeb was silent for a moment, then tapped Lex's arm. "He's got a carbine in his lap, boy. Remember what your paw said; not a sound." Jeb squinted his eyes. "You should've accepted Raul's knife. This is a place where a dagger's worth fifty guns."

Lex looked around and made a wry face, but old Jeb shook his head. He was obviously thinking that in this case ends clearly justified means.

They crawled ahead until the land suddenly broke away east and west leaving them upon the spine of a long, flinty ridge, and here Lex abruptly halted, dropped flat and softly said, "Look west, Jeb, down below."

Jeb looked. There was another of those little grassy pot-holes down there, and in it were several people including what was obviously a girl with red-gold hair, a tan blouse and a long riding skirt.

Ward was there too, with both arms tight-lashed behind him. Those two were slightly apart from three big-hatted loafing Mexican raiders who were sitting cross-legged playing cards, probably Monte, the favorite gambling game of Mexico.

"You got your answer about how many of 'em there are," whispered Jeb. "Four, not six."

"Ward's tied, Jeb."

"Well I reckon," dryly said the older man. "He's twice as big as those greasers. They'd take no chances on him. Miss Jane isn't tied though."

Lex said nothing. He pulled his eyes away from that quiet scene below and concentrated upon the drowsing sentry on ahead. "Let's get him," he growled, "and get this over with."

EIGHT

They belly-crawled up to within several yards of the sentinel, got so close in fact they could make out every detail of his attire. He was not a young man although he was not yet as old as Jeb McCarty either. His face was the swarthy, flat and sinisterly dark face of a crossbreed Mexican.

"Yaqui," pronounced Jeb in a low whisper, meaning that Mexican looked more Yaqui Indian than Spanish. "They got eyes like eagles."

"I hope he hasn't got ears like one," said Lex thinly, suddenly disgusted with himself for refusing Raul's knife.

The raider had his back to a worn boulder and was indifferently gazing out over the immense landfall visible for hundreds of eastward miles from this height. He seemed drowsy, which was understandable; he had been in the saddle all the day before, all last night, and now, with a fresh day strengthening around him, that huge yellow disc in the sky was working its warmth deep into his muscles. Furthermore, as Lex lay there intently watching this man, he got the feeling that the raider was satisfied he and his friends were quite safe.

"Want to draw straws?" whispered Jeb. Lex shook his head, dropped back down and very carefully sketched out in his mind the route he'd take to get up behind that sentinel. Westward, on his left, there was a strong stand of pointed boulders, so he was safe from detection by those idling marauders down in the little grassy meadow. On ahead he would be safe too, right up to within five feet of the Mexican. Beyond that though, there was a flattened place with pulverized gravel intervening. This posed no great peril because by the time he got that close—if he got that close—he'd have to spring upon the man anyway. He looked around, caught old Jeb intently watching him, and made a rueful little grin. The old cowboy put his head close and said, "Never scorn a knife, boy. Knives are like whisky; they got their uses too."

"Wish me luck," said Lex, and began crawling away. The sun was well on its overhead way by now; it burnt with a hazy intensity turning the heavens brassy-blue and faded. Northward, eastward and southward, a misty haze began to form far out, to soften the land-form's forbidding harshness and obscure its great distances. It was not yet nine o'clock so that heat, although it was steadily building up, still lacked a lot of being as breathless as it would become by high noon.

But Lex would be no more sweat-drenched by noon than he was now, as he inched his way ahead with extreme caution, stopping only when blinding perspiration ran down into his eyes with its salty burn and annoyance.

He heard the onward Mexican shift position, clear his throat and expectorate. He was thirty feet off when that happened. He was only ten feet off when he heard the man grope around behind him, lift a canteen and gulp down lukewarm water, re-cap the canteen and set it gratingly back in the meager shade again. Then the Mexican belched and spat again.

He was behind the last boulder separating him from the sentinel when he distantly heard a horse whinny. He cursed fiercely and silently because he knew the Mexican would be jarred abruptly wide awake by that sound. When he risked a peek around the base of his shielding boulder he saw that this was so; the Mexican was shading his eyes with one hand peering intently into the broken land below him, his thick body stiffly erect and the hand upon his lapped carbine firm-gripped.

Lex drew back, took several long, deep breaths, and waited. He had no idea when one of those card-players down there would decide to climb up here and relieve his friend. For all he knew one of them might be coming up right now. He risked another little peek, saw that the Mexican was leaning with his thick shoulders settled against that backdrop boulder again, and made his decision. He drew his .45, got both legs up under him for the spring, ground his boot-heels flat down into the ancient shale, raised up just enough to catch one fast glimpse of the sentinel, then hurled himself forward.

The Mexican sensed rather than saw, peril, off on his left. He tried to whip around, to gather himself to leap upright and meet it, but he was handicapped by his carbine and by his relaxed sitting posture. He was half up off the ground twisting sideways when Lex struck him head on with all his considerable heft and solid weight behind that strike. The Mexican dropped his Winchester, staggered back and his shoulders struck unrelenting rock with savage force. But he was a tough, resourceful man, inured to violence and physical pain. That hurtling big body half-knocked the breath from him, but he still twisted to throw a solid fist and connect.

Lex felt the numbness from that blow travel down his right side. It told him in a second that this was no ordinary brawler he was locked in with. He used one elbow to batter the Mexican's exposed middle. He caught the man's ornate little short jacket and wrenched him around with his other hand traveling no more than fifteen inches to meatily sink into the same exposed belly. The Mexican, with his mouth open to cry out, gavc a soundlcss howl as thc wind broke out of him from that belly-strike.

Lex yanked the man savagely upright, saw his muddy dark eyes begin to aimlessly roll, and slammed him fiercely against the backgrounding boulder again, struck him in the face, struck him in the middle, dropped his left hand from the man's jacket and crossed his left over his right with two short, blasting blows that chopped downward with the full impact of a swung sledge. The Mexican's head snapped back, connected with granite, and made a crunching sound.

Lex eased back on his haunches. Neither of them had at any time been fully upright. Mostly, their battle had taken place while both were sitting or kneeling.

The Mexican's nose and mouth dripped claret. He hung suspended in a drooping position with his head lolling and his breathing audibly bubbling. He was totally unconscious and would remain that way for a very long time.

Lex disarmed the man but forgot to search his boot-top for the inevitable knife. But the moment Jeb crawled up he tore at the man's tight *charro* pant-leg, exposed the ivory handle of a razor-like stiletto, stuffed the thing into his belt and raised up to strike at dust upon his clothing and somberly examine the wreckage of their enemy.

"When you hit 'em," he gravely said, "they sure stay hit. Better lash his legs and arms and gag him. He probably won't be comin' around for a long while but we got too big a set of stakes in this game to take chances."

They used the Mexican's clothing to fashion bonds and left the man limply under that pitiless sun as they slipped on around to the jagged-spired edge of this high place and make a long, silent study of the lower-down place where Ward and Jane Adair sat apart from those card-playing other Mexicans.

"You go back," said Jeb, finally, "and bring up the others. I'll stay here an' watch."

Lex was doubtful. Old Jeb was tough, he was wily, but he was at least twenty-five years older than any of those lean desert wolves down there; sooner or later one of them, perhaps more than one, would come trudging up to relieve their friend at the sentinel peak.

Lex shook his head.

"You go back. I'll keep watch up here."

Old Jeb understood perfectly and bared his teeth in a cold smile. He reached around, drew forth that ivory-handled boot-knife and wiggled it so that sunlight bitterly glinted off it. "Son, I know you got no use for these things, but I reckon today you learnt they're a lot better'n a .45 in certain situations. Well now, I never told you this before but I'll sure tell you now—I've had occasion more than once to use one of these things in my lifetime, an' those three down there, as long as they don't all come at me at once, an' don't know I'm up here, will be like sittin' ducks, as long as I got this here blade and the advantage of them not knowin' I'm here. So go on, and don't you worry about old Jeb McCarty. You just worry about not fallin' into that danged canyon down there or makin' a lot of noise. But hurry."

Lex left. It took him longer to get back down off the rim than it afterwards took him to get back where the others were sweatily waiting. He could be spotted from below upon the rim, but when he was down on the trail again, since that hawk-eyed sentinel was no longer able to cause trouble, he broke over into a swift trot and ran all the way back where his father, Pifas, Raul Hernandez, and the other men from Morgan Ranch were silently and sweatily standing around.

Old Hyatt sprang up off the rock wall he was leaning upon as soon as Raul hissed that someone was approaching. The moment Lex came swiftly around to them Hyatt loosened in his stance and looked enormously relieved.

"Did you find the watcher?" he demanded.

"We found him," reported Lex, "and he's trussed like a turkey and unconscious."

"Then let's go," stated his father, starting past.

"Wait a minute," exclaimed Lex. "Ward and Jane are up there with three more Mex raiders. They're all of them down in a little hollow in plain sight. No trees or nearby rocks for those men to hide behind."

"Well then," exclaimed old Hyatt impatiently, and got sharply cut off by Lex.

"Will you wait a minute, dammit!" Lex glared at his father and old Hyatt subsided. "Listen to me, all of you: Jeb is atop the ridge overlooking that pot-hole where Ward and the others are. I don't think we should go back up that same way."

"How then?" asked Hyatt, turning interested finally.

"I think we can find a way around that meadow to flank those raiders. I think we've got to, because if we simply go back up where Jeb and I were and start shooting, those raiders are going to kill Ward and Jane. We've got to completely cut them off, not only from their horses, which won't be hard, but also from getting through these hills southward or westward too. That way, I think, when they know there's not a chance, they'll try to use Ward and Jane as a means for buying their way clear."

Old Hyatt and Epifanio exchanged a look. Epifanio solemnly nodded. Raul Hernandez said quietly, "One man can watch their horses from the trail. It is much higher than that little place where the animals are. He could pick off anyone sliding down into that place like shooting prairie dogs." Raul cocked his head at Lex. "Is Jeb upon the rim overlooking the meadow where the people are?"

"Yeah; in the rocks up there, Raul."

"Then he can stop them from trying to climb out that way; no?"

"That's right. That's what I'm tryin' to tell you fellers," replied Lex. "The rest of us have got to cut them off southward and westward. It won't take long to cover the southward routes out of there, but whoever goes on westward to flank them will have a long way to go."

Hernandez smiled at Lex. "You and I," he said. "We can trot like Apaches."

Lex swung towards his father. Hyatt said nothing, he only nodded. Lex stepped away, turned, and with the carbine in his fist which Epifanio had handed him, began retracing his way.

There was no great need for caution now. Not until, up near the rimrocks, they were separated from the lower-down marauder-hideout by one curving, long ridge of that same spiny higher-up place where old Jeb still lay.

They left a *vaquero* secreted in rocks overlooking the little watered pot-hole where the raiders had left their animals. They trotted along past the catclaw and nopal clumps, past those spiny, golden-bloomed paloverdes, past that abrupt drop-off where Lex and Jeb had been compelled to drop down a nearly sheer cliff-face and inch their way along, and ultimately they came to the trail-side rise where the rimrocks rose up gradually off on their right towards that spot where the sentinel had been, and where old Jeb still was, lying hidden and watchful in the rocks.

Here, they halted and old Hyatt asked several quick questions: Did Raul know the onward country? Raul said that he did. Was Lex sure the raiders didn't suspect anything yet? Lex was sure. "Then," said old Hyatt, "let's get on with this. Lex, you an' Raul start ahead. Pifas, you and the remaining men scatter out in the draws and little canyons southward. I'll angle along the rocks until I find Jeb. We'll keep 'em from gettin' out of here the way they came in."

NINE

Lex and Raul Hernandez left at once, following game trails where they existed, making their own trails where none others were available. Because they had the farthest distance to traverse these two trotted along, slowing only when the terrain made this mandatory. Sweat ran off them in rivulets, catclaw clumps tore their clothing and once, when they inadvertently jumped across a shallow ravine, a startled rattlesnake made his warning noise at them both.

The sun was almost directly overhead now. It was well past ten o'clock, much closer to eleven. That heat was becoming sulphurous and shimmery, the hills, canyons, even the shadowy places, began to writhe and dance.

Lex led although probably Raul Hernandez, who knew this country better, should have been leading. Still, where Lex had instantaneous decisions to make, he never faltered and because he was acutely conscious of the necessity of speed, they kept moving.

Primarily, all Lex had to do was keep noise to a minimum and keep a shielding barrier of ridges and rims between he and Raul, and that northward place where the raiders and their hostages were. Neither of these things were especially difficult to achieve. Still, it took the pair of them a full hour to get across the land westerly, then swing northward a half-mile into some rocks above and behind the raider-camp. By then it was almost unbearably hot.

Lex sank limply down behind a three-foot-high boulder, rested for two minutes, then cautiously twisted around, raised up and peered downward. Beside him, Raul did the same. They both hung like that, with only the tops of their hatless heads visible, for a long time.

Raul swore in Spanish and said, "There are only two; where is the third one?"

Lex was searching for that one also. He had his brother, Jane Adair, and the two visible Mexicans in plain sight, but where there had been five people down there in that exposed, bitterly hot place, now there were only four.

He peered straight across at the opposite sidehill thinking he might pick out something climbing upwards over there, below where he'd left old Jeb. But there was no movement, no shadow of a man, no nothing at all but gelatin heat-waves quivering upwards over that entire heat-blasted place of rock.

"We've got to wait," he said, dropping back down beside Raul. "I hope to hell the others also wait."

"He may have another way of going to the horses," suggested Raul, and wrinkled his brow trying to recall if such a pathway existed.

"No," said Lex. "He's up the rocks somewhere trying to sleep maybe."

"What can we do, then?" asked the *vaquero*. "I don't believe the others are going to wait for ever, *Señor.*"

"They'd better," growled Lex, turning over, raising up for another downward look. "One shot now and I don't think anyone will walk out of that canyon."

They waited and watched and copiously perspired. Neither of them had a canteen and thirst began to be a constant torment. In this wild desert many a man had perished after being fully exposed to the sun without water after only one day. Salt formed on their hides beneath their shirts, making arm-movement painful around armpits, and also making their skin turn extremely sensitive each time they breathed and cloth grated over flesh. Still, that third Mexican did not reappear.

Lex's mind tormented him too. He knew the others were in place, that his father had found Jeb by this time and would be impatiently lying up there with his carbine following those two raiders down there. Jeb would be able to dissuade old Hyatt, but those *vaqueros* who had crept down into the southward breaks with Epifanio, were not nearly as likely to be dependable; not feeling as they were and had been feeling ever since entering these forbidding hills.

There was the chance too, that the missing marauder might be skirting somewhere around through the northward rocks on his way up to relieve that beaten sentinel. If this were so, then he might conceivably flank Hyatt and Jeb. Then, regardless of the best intentions of those two men over there, gunfire would surely ensue.

"We've got to chance it," said Lex suddenly, and began edging downhill towards the rocks at the base of that green spot where the raiders and their unsuspecting hostages were.

Raul said softly, "It makes for great danger, friend," in his strange-sounding Spanish.

Lex ignored this, glided on downhill aware that Jeb and his father could see him, could see Raul too where the *vaquero* also went cautiously from boulder to boulder, and he was sure the older men would do nothing yet.

It took them twenty minutes to get down that boulder-slope almost to the little meadow. Heat rose up around them like an invisible force, pressing upon them, sucking perspiration out and drying it before it touched their clothing, interfered with their vision too, and made perspective fade until there was no dimensional difference to distances.

Where they halted the last time behind a huge, cracked old horse-high stone, Raul ran a drying tongue around his lips and shook his head. "Like hell," he muttered. "Like purgatory down here."

Lex looked out, saw how Jane and his brother were wilting under that merciless overhead sun, saw how those two Mexicans were sitting further back in shadeless lethargy, and decided it was time to call out, regardless of where that other man was.

Then it came: a flat-echoing solitary gunshot far southward!

Both those lethargic marauders on across the little meadow whipped upright off the ground in a second, their carbines swinging southward with their turning bodies.

But there was only that one gunshot. In this echoless, lead-heavy atmosphere the silence dropped down again with smothering weight, everything was as before within moments, but those two raiders were thoroughly aroused now. One spoke a crisp order to the other. That second man turned at once and started across towards the hostages.

Neither Jane nor Ward Morgan had moved when that shot had sounded, except to raise their heads, to look southward. Now, that Mexican walked over, stepped behind those two with clear meaning, and halted back there holding his carbine loosely lifted and ready to fire. The Mexicans had an ironic name for it, shooting someone in the back of the head like this, when their arms were bound and their attention was diverted.

Lex held his breath and scarcely breathed.

"He will not do it now," whispered Raul. "Not until the other one comes back. Watch that one, *Señor,* he is walking south."

They watched. That other Mexican was moving along fully exposed but with his carbine poised and his head alertly up and moving. Where the sidehill obstructed further sight and movement, the raider briefly halted, looked carefully all around, then started climbing upwards.

"Ah," sighed Raul Hernandez putting aside his Winchester. "That one belongs to me." He started to glide off. Lex reached out and detained him.

"You stay still," he ordered. "Pifas and the others are down there some place. Let them have him. But first he's got to get out of sight of his friend up there standing behind Ward."

Raul subsided, but his slitted black eyes never stopped watching the marauder; there were little firepoints of murderous light glowing in their depths.

Gradually, with what to Lex was excruciating slowness, that panting Mexican made his way up the southward sidehill. He halted for a long time while still a hundred feet below the top-out, and for the last time he turned to gaze far back where his companion still stood behind Ward Morgan and Jane Adair, ready in a second to kill them both. Then that man started slogging his way uphill, reached the top and halted up there, a perfect target, to look for a long moment southward, eastward, and westward.

That was when the second shot came. Lex heard it and wrenched stiffly forward expecting for that exposed *bandido* to drop. But the Mexican didn't even flinch; he instead seemed suddenly to turn to stone as he peered intently down beyond his vantage point southward.

"He's seen them," whispered Raul. "He's seen Pifas or one of the others down there."

Lex was not so sure of that. For one thing, the raider made no move to drop down which Lex was positive he would have done had he spotted anyone unknown to him within rifle-range. For another, instead of lowering his head or even raising his carbine, the man stood there looking far ahead and slightly upwards along the southerly rims.

"No, Raul; that gunshot came from a long way off. Besides, watch his head. He's not looking down into the rocks; he's looking further out."

"Then," demanded Raul, "who is shooting?"

Lex did not attempt an answer because he was as mystified as the *vaquero* was about this. Several ideas passed through his mind; perhaps, out where the stolen herd was being driven along, the other marauders had run into trouble. Possibly a patrol of Arizona Rangers had come across them. Perhaps it was simply a band of cowmen out hunting strays who had come across the Morgan herd, recognized the

Morgan brand, and who had surmised at once what those Sonora-Mexicans were doing with it, and had attacked them running them back up into these hills.

But in the end Lex accepted none of these doubtful notions and said only, "I don't know who fired those shots, but I think we'd better make our play before that feller turns and signals for his friend to shoot my brother and Miss Jane."

Lex was gathering himself to rise up when Raul gasped and pointed. *"El Patron,"* he said. "Your father, *Señor.*"

Lex sprang up in full view and looked slightly northward where old Hyatt's unmistakable big form rose silently up from the sidehill-boulders less than a hundred yards from that Mexican standing down there behind the prisoners. He called out and his words carried in that insufficient, hot air all the way across to where Lex and Raul Hernandez stood like stone.

"Vaquero!"

The marauder's head whipped sideways. He saw old Hyatt over there with his carbine up and snugged back, with his grizzled old grey head lowered lethally sighting down the carbine barrel, and the Mexican froze with his own gun barrel no more than six feet behind Ward Morgan's head, his dark trigger-finger tightly curled.

"Put down the gun," said old Hyatt. "Lower it very carefully or I'll kill you by inches."

Lex held his breath. At his side Raul Hernandez said, "The other one, *Señor;* the one on the ridge. Look."

Lex looked. The second raider was turned, facing downward. He could also see what was happening down in the little heat-shimmering green place, but he was much too far away to do anything about it, so he stood up there like a graven image waiting, as Lex and Raul also were waiting, and even old Jeb up in his shielding, furnace-hot rock pile was waiting too, for that Mexican to make his decision.

Hyatt spoke again in that same frigid, completely deadly tone, saying to the Mexican standing behind Ward: "First through the belly, *vaquero,* then through the jaw, then through the spine. You will not die for two, maybe three days, if you pull that trigger, but by the Sacred Lord of Heaven you will surely meet your Maker."

Old Hyatt's Spanish was graphic and bell-clear. It was also, along with Hyatt's unmistakable stance, very convincing; slowly the perspiring Mexican lowered his carbine.

Ward got heavily upright turning towards his father as he did so. Jane stepped over to his side and began to at once work at the lashings holding Ward's arms behind him. The Mexican standing with them bent, carefully put down his Winchester, straightened back up again and turned to fully face old Hyatt. He said something indistinguishable to Lex and Raul in Spanish and stretched out both his hands in a supplicating manner.

Lex let all his breath rush out. He put forth a hand to steady himself, scarcely felt the searing burn from the hot rock his palm lighted upon, and swung to gaze up where the other Mexican had been atop the ridge. He was no longer there.

"I can still get him," said Raul quietly, considering that southward ridge.

"No; leave him to the others. Come on; let's go down there."

They walked on down into the little grassy place, started on across and saw Hyatt also walking outwards. From far up the eastward spine where he'd been lying old Jeb suddenly sprang up and cried out. Lex and Raul halted to peer overhead but old Hyatt acted as though he hadn't heard; he kept right on walking.

"What's he doing?" asked Raul Hernandez perplexedly.

"Signaling," snapped Lex, and started to spin off in the northerly direction old Jeb was frantically pointing. Lex hadn't completed that turn when the flat, harsh smash of a gunshot broke the heavy silence.

Jane screamed. It was like a steel nail being scraped up the raw nerves of every man who heard that outcry.

Raul also cried out. He started running forward. Lex whipped back around just in time to see his brother wilt, slump forward, take two unsteady steps towards old Hyatt, and fall flat down.

Jeb was firing now, over their heads northward into a boulder-field in that direction. Raul dropped to one knee and also fired into those rocks. Lex started running ahead, over towards his brother.

Old Hyatt got there first, dropped down and picked up his youngest son's head, cradled it in his corded old arms and held it. He never once looked up to see that Jane Adair was safe or what the firing was about where Raul and Jeb were thunderously shooting.

Suddenly the last shot was fired. Jeb was flinging himself along his spiny ridge heading for the spot where that third raider, the one they had never been able to locate, had suddenly risen up to shoot Ward Morgan.

Raul Hernandez was much closer so he got over there first. He was in among those boulders a long time before he re-emerged dragging with him the corpse of that third Mexican. The man was dead; he had one bullet-hole in his smashed left shoulder, but what had dispatched him was the series of savage punctures across the chest where Raul Hernandez's knife had done its silently lethal work.

Lex did not yet know any of this. By the time he got over to his father and brother Jane was also kneeling in that fiercely hot place, her face white to the hairline, her eyes dry and stricken and unmoving. When Lex sank down she didn't look at him. Neither did old Hyatt. It was as though both of those people were completely unaware of anything except the dead face of young Ward Morgan, there in his father's arms.

TEN

A half-hour later Epifanio and the other *vaqueros* came scrambling over the ridge separating that green little place from the southward twists and turns where they had been hiding. They walked the last hundred yards without speaking, their attention fixed upon dead Ward Morgan in his father's arms.

Raul Hernandez went over and cautioned them into silence, then the lot of them stood respectfully back a little distance and removed their hats.

Old Jeb was the last one to get down there. He had detoured to go over and inspect the sniper Raul Hernandez had killed. He also walked up behind the solitary marauder left alive and yanked away this man's holstered .45, which he pitched over into the rocks.

Jane went back to the little rock-clump where she and Ward had spent the day and sank down over there. She did not cry, did not make a single sound of any kind. She simply went away from the others and sat down oblivious to that blasting sun, to the presence of all those men, and to her own physical faintness.

Old Hyatt was a long time without moving, but eventually he raised glazed eyes and said to Raul Hernandez, "Did you kill the one who did this?"

"Si, patron."

"Then," said the old man very softly, "kill the other one too."

Raul turned and at once started off. For just a second none of the others thoroughly understood what was going to happen, but that brief moment passed and they watched Hernandez in fascinated horror. Old Jeb stood by the prisoner with his mouth slack. Epifanio, and the *vaqueros* standing back with him, had not heard the order given by Hyatt but they understood at once the unmistakable stalk of Raul Hernandez and stared in disbelief.

The solitary surviving marauder had neither fully understood Hyatt's order to Raul, given in English, nor Hernandez's purpose in heading for him, until Raul was close enough for the bandit to read his expression. Then the man cried out in Spanish for mercy. Raul did not slacken pace. The Mexican rolled his eyes, saw old Jeb and hesitated a moment before he abruptly turned and began to run.

Lex, down on both knees beside his father and his dead brother, only roused himself when that bandit cried out. He lifted his head, turned and looked out where Raul was springing swiftly after the fleeing man. He seemed not to quite grasp what was happening out there.

Hernandez caught the marauder just short of that same jumble of rocks where Ward Morgan's assassin had been dozing when the men of Morgan Ranch had appeared, and where that assassin had fired that fatal shot. He struck the Mexican with his open hand first, they all saw that and understood its purpose—Raul was counting coup first, he struck an enemy with his open hand to show bravery—then he tripped the Mexican and threw himself downward.

The desperate marauder twisted away, he lashed out with one hand to knock his executioner aside, he scrambled half over and got upon feet in a wild upright lunge. Raul caught one ankle and threw the

Mexican down again. It struck everyone who was stonily watching that Hernandez was playing with the raider.

Lex sprang up with horror in his expression. He opened his mouth to call out, but Hernandez rolled sideways, came up over the threshing, arching, straining Mexican, and his right hand flashed up and down, up and down. It was all over. Lex still stood there, lips parted, as Raul got up, sheathed his boot-knife, beat dust from himself and turned his back upon the dead marauder.

Old Hyatt had seen none of it; he didn't raise his head until Lex dropped to one knee staring at him, and said, "That was murder pure and simple. He wasn't even armed."

Hyatt looked up from where he still crouched, sweat-sodden, his clothing torn and soiled, his craggy face yellowish-grey and grief-tortured. "You can't murder a murderer," he retorted, in a voice roughened by anguish. "We're going to kill every one of them." Old Hyatt looked over, saw Epifanio standing apart, hat in hand, and said, "Go bring on our horses."

Pifas left with two men, Raul Hernandez sauntered back and halted nearby saying nothing and avoiding the stares of his fellow *vaqueros* as well as the suddenly abhorrent stare of Jeb McCarty and Lex. He stood easy, both thumbs hooked in his shell-belt; clearly, in his own mind, Raul Hernandez had done no wrong.

Hyatt got up very stiffly, put his hat over Ward's

drying eyes, glanced dully around at the others, let his gaze linger a moment upon Jane Adair out where she sat wilted and terribly quiet, then he dropped his eyes to Lex. "You and Raul go after that other one. The one that walked out over that southward ridge. He'll be with friends by now maybe; it was one of them on horseback far southward who fired that shot a while back, signaling I think, because another one even further southward also fired one shot. You two go find that one. The rest of us will come along behind you."

"Listen," said Lex in quick protest, "you can't take Miss Jane down through this country. It's too hot an' she's been through too much already."

"She'll go back to the ranch with Ward. Now you an' Raul get your horses and go along, Lex, an' when you find 'em try an' get below 'em southward. Cut 'em off from the border. I want every one of those raiders. If you can't cut 'em off, then get that one who left this place, and keep the others in sight until we find you." Old Hyatt jerked his head. "Now leave."

Raul walked over beside Lex and waited out that moment while father and son stared at one another, and as Lex suddenly turned away, Raul went along with him silently and obediently. As the two of them walked past the other *vaqueros* Raul smiled at them. Not a man smiled back. Raul's smile grew a little strained, he shrugged and walked on.

Lex met Epifanio on the uphill trail bringing down their animals. At sight of Raul, Epifanio rolled his eyes in what could have been dismay but which was probably disapproval. Lex retrieved his animal, borrowed a carbine from one of the men with Epifanio, explained where he'd left his own carbine, then told Epifanio what he and Raul had been sent to do.

Old Epifanio rolled his eyes again, and this time it clearly *was* dismay. *"Señor,"* he breathed in soft Spanish, "your father asks a formidable thing of you—his sole remaining son. There will be eight or perhaps ten of those riders of other people's horses, and we will be many fewer."

Hernandez eyed old Epifanio wryly and also said in Spanish, "The patron gives orders, his children obey. It is that simple old one. Please; the reins to my horse."

The reins were passed over. Epifanio considered Raul for a second then sadly wagged his head. "What a man is the first ten years of his life, friend, is evidently what he then becomes and remains. Is this not so?"

"One pronouncer against law and order," retorted Raul, mounting up and half-smiling down at the older man. "What is such a life, old one; something to be respected or obliterated? That one would assuredly have killed the patron's youngest anyway; this much was obvious as he stood back there with his cocked carbine. No, old one, in the missions you have learned a bad thing—a fatal thing. If you do not kill those who should die, they will ultimately kill you. My conscience is very clear."

"Well then," said old Pifas with a big shrug, his

words coming still in soft Spanish, "since we all are sinners, we all deserve to die." Epifanio looked upwards steadily, and as Lex also stepped up over leather the old *vaquero* said to the younger one, "I will remember what we have said here, young one, and from this day on you will never get behind me again."

Pifas and his companion started on along the trail leading their horses. Raul looked after them briefly and Lex watched him, beginning to lose some of the numbness which had gripped him since the murder of his brother, beginning to wonder if one thing in particular that old Epifanio had said was not the truth: that whatever a man is as a child, he remains all his life. Raul Hernandez, stolen as a baby and raised by Apache customs, might in every outward respect be an American of Mexican descent, but actually he was an Apache with all the fierce and savage convictions of the people who had raised him.

Lex was lifting his reins to turn off southward when a corollary thought struck him, and struck him hard. His own father had come to early manhood in the violent, savage Texas of a generation ago; his convictions, like those of Raul Hernandez, had been entirely shaped by a way of life which was fast passing, and yet his father and Raul Hernandez would not change. Neither of them had seen anything at all either immoral or illegal in the execution of that unarmed raider from Sonora.

Lex turned his horse and rode along with Raul behind him. Where he came to a sloping sidehill he cut southward down it and sat his tilted saddle letting the horse slither and slide through foot-deep shale to the arroyo's bottom before guiding him through a narrow place where a suffocating welter of disturbed heat-waves rose up around them. He neither halted nor looked back. He went along turning some strange thoughts over and over in his mind.

It took the pair of them quite a little while to get over into that broken, brushy country south of the place where his brother had died. By then there was beginning to be a trace of pale shadows here and there, upon the east side of brush patches and boulders.

From this place, which was below the ridge where they had last seen that survivor of the raider band before he'd fled, the land began to noticeably alter. There was spiny sage and buckbrush down here, some nopal and catclaw too. It was a place where enormous, hairy tarantula spiders and hungry rattlers lived, and occasionally they came upon signs that deer foraged this brushy land.

On their right were low hills but on their left were the same type of jagged, rocky upthrusts which had been everywhere around them further back. Lex kept watching the gentler swells off on the right. Up there, somewhere, if his deductions were correct, had been where that Mexican on the ridge had seen something when he'd stood so long staring upward and westward. There would be game trails up there through the underbrush. Without saying a word he dropped his gaze, kept watch for an angling-upwards trail, and when he found one some hundred yards on along, he took it, heading for the higher ground.

It was rough going; for deer that trail was adequate, but for mounted men it was too narrow. Their legs and saddles constantly got raked by thorny growth, deer-flies rose up eagerly to explore their ears and nostrils, sweat ran and the heat bore against them with solid pressure.

Lex halted finally, half-way up towards the top-out of those westerly knolls. He stepped down to rest his horse and watched Raul also dismount. The little *vaquero* looked over and said, "I think the raiders with the herd sent two men back here to find the others and to bring them along. Why else would there be two of them, one behind the other, and each of them signaling ahead with a gunshot?"

Lex drank from his canteen, capped the thing and slung it back over his saddlehorn. He had long since arrived at the same conclusion Raul had just expounded, so all he said was, "If they haven't too big a head-start maybe we can overtake them."

Raul looked doubtful of this but he did not disagree. He shot a long, considering glance on up where the rim was, and studied it in total silence for a long while.

Lex remounted, said, "Remember, Raul, if the man who got away, got to his friends, one of those horses will be carrying double. In a place like this, under that sun, no horse made can move fast or far under those conditions. Come on; let's move out."

They made the top-out with the off-center sun beginning to faintly redden. It was cooler up atop the high ground, and they almost immediately came across the tracks of a shod horse. This animal had been coming northward at a steady walk. Then he'd halted, and here they found the shiny brass casing of an expended .45 shell.

Lex tossed the thing to Raul. "Where the raider fired that first shot we heard."

They traced out where that horse had reversed itself and had gone back over its own earlier tracks, southward again. They also found where a man on foot had come crawling up onto the trail from the brushy sidehill. Here, they could read from the sign how two men had stood beside a quiet horse talking back and forth, how the man on foot had squatted down from exhaustion, and later, how the two of them had then got astride the rider's animal and had resumed their southward way.

Raul read even more from those footprints than Lex did. He pointed out where the afoot-man had turned northward. "He was pointing back where he'd come from," said Hernandez. "He was explaining to his friend what was happening down in the little green place. They stood there listening to the gunfire, then they rode on." Raul shot a look at the reddening sun, shot a longer look straight southward where their upland trail ran along, and he said thoughtfully, "I think we can catch them both long before sundown."

As they mounted Lex motioned for Hernandez to

come up and ride stirrup with him. When the two of them were side by side Lex said, "Raul, you will do exactly as I tell you from now on."

Hernandez looked across with surprise on his face. "*Si*," he murmured. "Of course; here, you are *el jefe*—the chief, and I will obey."

"Then you will not knife that man who ran away."

"*Señor*, your father said—"

"My father isn't up here, I am. Is that clear?"

"Yes, it is clear."

They rode southward saying no more, their eyes constantly searching the onward land.

ELEVEN

Dusk would not come to the summer-time desert until nine o'clock in the night. What Raul thought probable was entirely possible. Lex knew this when they found where that second horseman, the one who had been a mile behind the first rider and who had also fired a signal-shot, had stood beside his animal, waiting and watching the northward land.

Here again, Raul Hernandez read the sign with Apache-trained eyes. "This one saw the other two coming and waited. Here, you see where he smoked two cigarettes—there are the stubs. *Señor*, a man does not smoke two cigarettes one after the other, so there was a long interval."

"What of it?" asked Lex.

"*Señor*, that second horse, the one carrying two men,

was traveling very slow. This second man had a long wait. That means that the three of them are still moving along very slowly and we can catch them."

Lex found no fault with this logic as they got back astride and rode onward. He concentrated upon watching the southerly landforms. There was that same brushy canyon on their left, and further out in the same direction, that same north-to-south flow of jagged ramparts which cut off all view of the westward world. They could have been the only two people in the world; there was no sign of any movement, any life at all of any kind, wherever they looked. But underfoot, upon this same broad trail they were riding, were those tell-tale shod-horse marks.

A mile onward they saw a scraggly pine tree. Further along were other trees; the land was changing again, becoming less barren and astringent. Raul lifted his arm to indicate a heat-hazed distant hillside, and say, "There is better country up there. Once, when I was small, I spent a whole summer up there in camp beside a blue lake. From among those forests one can see a long way down into Mexico."

"I know the place," Lex said dryly. "Once we chased a band of horse-stealing Indians up in there."

Raul dropped his arm and rode silently along after that.

The country dipped low into a big saddle before it began its ultimate climb to those lofty, timbered heights, and it was just before they left the uplands to pass down into that huge swale that Hernandez made a short grunt and jutted with his chin.

"There are the raiders," he softly said, indicating a very distant, very faint-seen shadow of movement starting up along the far side of the swale.

Lex didn't see them for another ten minutes, but then he had never learned how to block in miles of emptiness with unmoving eyes, so that when anything moved it at once showed forth in a glaring manner. When he finally did spy those riders he kept riding along watching them for a long while before he spoke.

"Their animals are tiring, Raul. I reckon they'll have to rest in the trees."

But Hernandez had already seen that this was so and had been searching for a way westerly down off this brushy trail where they would eventually be seen the same way they had spotted those Mexicans—by movement. He pointed to a narrow buck-run leading down the far side of the hills on their right.

"Down there, *jefe,*" he murmured. "At the bottom we'll find other trails. We can keep this ledge between us and them and get up close before they suspect we are anywhere around."

Lex nodded and left the main trail. The moment his horse began bucking brush again, it threw up its head in disapproval. Lex kept right on going and before they got fully down the hill and located another trail bearing southward, the horse had become reconciled to discomfort.

There was no shade on this side of the hills; the westering sun burnt redly against them but some of its heat had diminished so the going-along was not too uncomfortable. Lex drank, slung his canteen around the horn and wished for a smoke. He was hungry too, but hunger was something he'd long ago learned to live with. Behind him, Raul also sipped from a canteen and slouched along. One thing a man learned in this lethal summer-time land was to move as little as possible while riding through the heat of the day, to put worry and tension out of his mind, and to drink sparingly of water. These two did these things, and shortly before they came to the first pine tree upon the swale's northward, rising slope, they found a waterhole with greeny scum around its edges where they halted to water their animals and to make a quiet study of the uphill land ahead of them.

Here, for the first time since early morning, Raul smiled. It was a wolfish sort of smile. He said, "I know this country well, from here on. We can get completely around them without much trouble." Raul lowered his black gaze to Lex. "I think they must be heading for the blue lake. Or if not there, then for one of the grassy places on the west slope where they can sit up high in good shade and watch their stolen cattle down below in the big wash." Raul made a wide gesture with one upflung arm. "Mexico is not far from here. If the three men ahead do not get to their friends with the herd, I think we will be able to get beyond the rustlers as your father wished and keep them from getting over the border."

"We'd better prevent that," said Lex dryly. "Once

cattle get over the line into Mexico, no power on earth will bring them back."

Raul seemed to run this last statement of Lex's through his mind; he shrugged though, without comment, and when Lex got back into the saddle, Raul also stepped up.

"You go ahead," ordered Lex, and allowed the *vaquero* to take the lead as they resumed their way.

They had no way of knowing, now, because of the intervening mountains, whether the three raiders they were pursuing, were still moving or had halted up in the pine trees somewhere. But that didn't trouble either of them for the elemental reason that it was their desire to get beyond the Mexicans anyway. All that seemed to matter now to Raul Hernandez was that they cut those three riders off from a juncture with their friends. Lex was perfectly willing to have it this way too, at least until they got around the three marauders; after that he would reassume command.

The land began to sharply lift underfoot; a definite pine-fragrance permeated the otherwise breathless air, and finally, a half-hour later, Raul paused beneath a huge old pine tree and smiled at Lex from hot shade. They were now well up the southernmost slope. "We will go west from here," stated Raul. "We must find those riders again." As he squared back around in his saddle Hernandez said indifferently, "It will be shady from here on."

It was shady, too, but the shade itself was actually no cooler because of the increased humidity up in this forested place. It did, however, offer a pleasant change, and since it somewhat mitigated the sun's direct, fierce rays, it was a welcome change to Lex as he followed Raul along the sidehill, bearing off to their left.

Raul ultimately halted, got down and wordlessly tied his horse in a crowded stand of second-growth trees. He kept his eyes dead ahead, towards the west, and he also seemed to be listening. Lex dismounted, took his carbine and went along beside the *vaquero* when Hernandez began gliding silently in and out of the onward shadows. Here, thought Lex as he watched the cowboy, Raul Hernandez was finally fully reverted to what he'd come to manhood being—an Apache.

They came to a slightly open place upon the hillside which offered an excellent down-hill view. Raul halted, stood like a statue for a long moment, then relaxed, grounded his carbine and softly smiled.

"There," he exclaimed, "look downhill and to the right. There they are, sitting together in shade resting their animals."

Lex saw the marauders at once and was surprised that Hernandez's inherent sense of direction had brought them so accurately out above those men down there.

The raiders were smoking and idly watching the long stretch of open country northward. They were patently feeling very safe in their speckled shade, very secure from the pursuit they watched for and did not see.

"I think," murmured Raul, "that old Jeb will be leading your father and the others."

"Maybe," assented Lex, throwing a long look outward over the land they had just traversed.

"Because," went on the *vaquero,* "if it was old Pifas, he would bring them straight along that upland trail where those men below us would see their dust. But old Jeb is a coyote; he will know to keep down the west sidehill where there will be no dust and where those marauders can't see movement."

Lex looked over at the softly smiling younger man and wondered how he had arrived at this correct assessment of how wily old Jeb McCarty could be. As though suddenly aware of Lex's thoughts, Hernandez turned his head.

"Those old ones," he said, reverting to that peculiarly guttural Spanish of his, "are as clever as a fox and as fierce—-sometimes. They think always ahead, and they plan that way too." Hernandez shrugged, sank down with his Winchester between his knees and fell to watching the Mexicans below them and several hundred yards away.

Lex also sat down. He thought he knew what was going through his companion's head as Hernandez wolfishly watched those unsuspecting men further down the hill. Old Hyatt had said the raider who had escaped must be killed. Raul Hernandez was remembering that, and he was deciding which of those three men down there would be that particular one.

It was not difficult, even this far off, to tell which of

those men looked the most worn and dusty, the most scratched by thorns and sweaty from trotting away under a hot sun, from that place where his friends had all died.

"You just remember what I told you," Lex admonished quietly. "Up here, I give the orders."

Hernandez didn't look away from those men down below. He simply shrugged and sat on, relaxed, holding his carbine between his knees with both hands, motionless as stone, slit-eyed and as deadly as a mountain panther.

Lex tried to imagine what his father had done after he and Raul had left that green, small meadow where his brother had died. He also tried to imagine what arrangements had been made for getting Ward and Jane Adair back to the Morgan ranch. He considered it probable that his father had sent one or two of the *vaqueros* back with Jane and his brother's body, and if this were so, the Morgan men would be badly outnumbered by the raiders.

He also tried to guess how far back the others were. He meant to take those three unsuspecting marauders down the hill before they could ride on and meet their friends, but he earnestly wished he had some inkling where his father and the others were before he made his move.

Still, this knowledge was not available, so in the end he put it out of his mind, dropped his head and gazed down where those Mexicans were beginning to stir, were beginning to look as though they would very shortly mount up now and start onward.

Raul turned, after a while, gazed quietly at Lex as though awaiting orders, and said nothing until Lex got up and leaned upon his Winchester, obviously considering the best and safest way to do what they had come this far to accomplish.

Raul said: "*Jefe,* if we go westward a quarter mile we can get athwart their path. Then," Raul lifted his shoulders and let them fall, "either when we step out and order them to halt, they will do so, or they will start firing. And *jefe,* if they fire just one gun, their friends who are not far off now, will know what has happened—and everything will be undone."

Lex put a wry gaze upon the *vaquero*. He was remembering something old Jeb had said about there being times when one knife was worth fifty guns. "We'll take that chance," he murmured. "Lead out."

Raul turned at once and went cat-footing it along the sidehill towards a place where they could get ahead of the raiders. Below them, those three unsuspecting Mexicans also got astride and started along.

TWELVE

In every bad situation a man encounters in others the strengths and the weaknesses which go to make up human nature, and while he may disapprove of one, he can count himself lucky for the other. That's how it was with Lex as he allowed himself to be led swiftly through dark and light places in such a way that he was never once revealed to the three raiders he was pursuing. He could admire the strong characteristics possessed by Raul Hernandez which made this ambush possible, even while he also disapproved of the weakness in Hernandez's composite make-up which allowed the lithe *vaquero* to kill without qualms of any kind.

But it was the Apache-cunning which was currently prevailing, and to this Lex was thankful, for they got ahead of their enemies with no trouble at all, faded out in a wisely-selected place where underbrush grew amid tall old shaggy pines, and knelt down in there listening to the oncoming soft hoof-falls of two horses.

Raul was grinning again. his black eyes bright behind narrowed lids, his strong, white teeth showing starkly in the sun-layered darkness of his smooth face. In looking at the *vaquero,* Lex had time to feel a little chill, and wonder how many times, as a youth, Hernandez had done exactly as he was now doing, with a dozen bronco bucks, motionlessly waiting to spring upon and savagely massacre unsuspecting travelers.

Then Raul quietly sighed and Lex peered out through buck-brush branches and saw the foremost rider. This man was stocky, darkly swarthy, and had one shiny gold tooth set squarely in the middle of his upper jaw. He had the traditional crossed bandoleers with their wickedly glinting brass cartridges, and he also wore a tied-down six-gun on his right hip.

Directly behind the stocky marauder came the other

two astride the same horse. The man behind the saddle was faintly familiar to Lex, for although he'd never really seen this raider up close, the man's innate characteristics such as the way he carried his head, wore his hat, sat with his shoulders up and squared, were reminiscent of the way this same man had carried himself back in that lethal little meadow.

Raul tensed. Lex could feel this as Hernandez gripped his Winchester and swung a swift look around. Lex nodded and the brace of them abruptly rose up over the brush, raised their weapons and aimed them. They were separated from the three astonished Mexicans by no more than twenty feet.

The foremost man yanked his reins back and popped his eyes wide open. The second horseman, with his passenger on behind, had to also halt to prevent bumping into the foremost man. But this one was not so badly startled he did not react. As he dropped his right hand straight down Lex cocked his carbine. That moving hand suddenly stopped moving.

For a matter of several seconds there was not a move nor a sound. Lex let that time elapse purposefully; he wanted those Mexicans to understand how close to dying they were. Even brave men wilted when every recourse suddenly left them naked before death, and these three were not particularly brave men.

"Get down one at a time," Lex said in quiet Spanish. When each man had dismounted, was standing unnaturally stiff and shaken with those two carbine muzzles staring straight into their eyes, he said, using Spanish again, "With your left hands discard your pistols."

This order too was obeyed in absolute silence. The marauders now began to show their fright, their inevitable dismay. As they straightened up and looked over at Lex, transparent sweat began to bead their foreheads and upper lips.

"Go get their carbines, Raul," ordered Lex, lowering his own Winchester. "Don't get in front of them."

Hernandez moved lightly forward. He was grinning again. Those three captives looked away from Lex; they were clearly having some thoughts about this *vaquero* who moved and acted like an Apache, yet who obviously was of Mexican descent. As Raul disarmed each man he looked into his eyes with that little grin of his broadly showing; it was a calculated Apache trick to terrorize an unarmed enemy in this fashion, and it almost always worked. The raiders turned towards Lex with obvious supplication in their dark eyes.

When Raul finished gathering the guns he stepped back beside Lex. "That last one there, *jefe,* is the one we want."

Lex grounded his Winchester, stared at the indicated captive and without looking away he said, "We got him. We got all of them. Now you go back, fetch my horse down here, then you back-track and bring the others up here."

Raul didn't say a word of dissent, he caught up his carbine and went striding back the way they had come. Lex watched until Raul was lost from view among the pines, then returned his cold gaze to the prisoners.

"Where are the others?" he asked.

The foremost man lifted his hands, palms up, in a gesture indicating clearly that he understood no English. Lex was on the verge of repeating the question in Spanish when the rearmost Mexican said, "On around the mountainside, *Señor,* where it was arranged we should all meet again."

"With our cattle?" asked Lex.

The Mexican shook his head. "No, *Señor;* the cattle are down in that big arroyo. They cannot be moved again until sundown."

So far everything was as the Morgans had thought it would be. Lex looked steadily at that dusty, soiled and obviously worn-out man back there. "Your friends are dead," he said quietly. "You alone got out of that little valley alive."

"Si, Señor."

"That man who was with you; the one who went off into the rocks to sleep—he shot and killed your hostage, who was also my brother."

To this the Mexican said nothing, but his face perceptibly paled.

"That *vaquero* who was with me—he wanted to kill you. He was sent here to kill you for the murder of my brother."

Still that Mexican remained still and silent, but now he rolled his eyes around as though expecting to have Raul Hernandez abruptly appear with upraised knife.

A muscle in the side of his cheek twitched.

"What did you plan to do with my brother and the girl?"

The Mexican's hands fluttered. He said in an apologetic tone, "*Señor,* we only wanted a little ransom for the young man and the beautiful girl. It was not our intention to harm them."

"Then why did that man kill my brother, if it was not your intention to harm them?"

The sweating marauder made a helpless little shrug. "I don't know, *Señor.*"

"How long has your raider-band been in Arizona?"

"A few days only, *Señor.* We were in camp when one of the sentinels saw your herd coming. It was decided to stampede it south towards Sonora. We had no plan to take hostages for ransom until some of the men, while they slipped ahead to scout your herd, came upon the man and the beautiful girl out walking in the night. The men brought those two back, but our *capitan* didn't want them. He said it would be much safer if we ran off only the cattle. There was an argument—the *capitan* said those who wished to, could take the prisoners off into the hills and try to get ransom, but that the rest of the men must go southward with the cattle. We split up, *Señor,* at the first trail."

"I see," said Lex. "And you were one of those who decided to try for the ransom."

"*Si;* I will not deny it. But it was never my intention to see anyone hurt."

"Of course not," said Lex dryly. "Only to make them

sit out there in that killing sun without a canteen near them."

Raul returned astride his own animal and leading Lex's horse. After he had tied the riderless animal Raul turned in his saddle and put a steady, black stare back at that rearmost man. Lex saw that look and murmured, "Never mind. Head out now, find the others and bring them up here."

Raul looked down. "Maybe we ought to tie them. You are only one man and they are three."

Lex patted his holstered .45. "I am six men," he explained, with clear-enough meaning. "Six lead bullets in this gun. You go on, Raul, and make it fast."

The *vaquero* deliberately reined around and rode slowly down along the right side of those three stiff-standing prisoners, grinning again. Then he kicked out his animal and was shortly lost to sight.

"Sit down," ordered Lex. The three Mexicans dropped down. "Take off your hats and bandoleers." This order was also obeyed after that English-speaking raider had translated it. "I think you're going to spend the rest of your lives north of the border," Lex told the frozen-faced marauders. "Up here cattle rustling and murder are serious offences."

For some reason this seemed to please those captives after it had been translated to them. They began to relax, to look around them and over at one another. They seemed almost happy. The rumpled Mexican looked up at Lex and said, "*Señor,* that man who was with you—that one with the Indian smell to him—you will keep him away from us?"

Lex didn't answer. He sank down upon one knee, leaned upon his upright carbine and stoically regarded his prisoners. For the likes of these murderous, unwashed, villainous men, Ward had died, not as a man should die, but with both arms lashed behind him and within seconds of being saved.

He kept watching the heavily perspiring captives, his face deep-etched with tiredness and sorrow, with rancor and conflicting thoughts, and the time ran on.

Somewhere beyond the tallest tree that huge red disc was settling lower in the west. It was still a long time before dusk, but the shadows were firming up and the land was beginning to give off a steady rise of daytime heat.

It was pleasantly fragrant where he knelt. It was also utterly still. There were four men sitting there warily watching one another and not one of them offered to speak.

For two hours it was like that, then Lex heard the musical jangle of rein-chains and sprang upright. The Mexicans also stirred, swung their heads with hope and dread both, in their muddy eyes. When Raul Hernandez appeared, riding in and out among the trees, that hope faded and those sitting prisoners watched as other riders came quietly along behind Hernandez. By someone's order, probably old Hyatt's, Hernandez, old Jeb, Hyatt and the *vaqueros* bringing up the rear of the cavalcade, all rode with their carbines lying across their laps.

Raul stepped down, nodded at Lex, tied his horse and turned to seek out that particular marauder who had alone, survived out of that party back in the little canyon.

Hyatt came ahead with his Winchester in the crook of one arm. He paused before reaching Lex to cast a slow, milky stare over the cross-legged prisoners, then he passed along. Behind him old Jeb did the same, he walked up, looked down at the captives, then moved on. When the *vaqueros* came walking up Raul said to them in Spanish: "This is what you feared, back in the brushy canyon; this carrion."

The *vaqueros,* including Epifanio and numbering only four now, said nothing, woodenly regarded the prisoners, and stood off a little distance away from Hyatt and Lex and also away from Raul Hernandez.

Hyatt grounded his Winchester, considered Lex a moment then said, "Raul told me you wouldn't let him kill that last one over there."

Lex nodded affirmatively.

"Those men killed your brother, Lex."

"*That* one didn't."

The older man kept staring at his son. He said no more though, and after a while he drew back upright, looked around and said, "Jeb, you'n Pifas stay here with me. Raul, you'n Lex scout on around this side-hill. Find those other raiders, but don't let them even suspect you're anywhere around. Then hurry back here."

Old Hyatt shot Epifanio a careless look. "Tie these

murderers," he ordered, bobbing his head at the prisoners. "Tie their ankles, lash their arms behind 'em, and rip an arm out of each shirt to gag 'em with. We don't want anyone trying to cry out or run off. Be sure it's a good job, Pifas."

Epifanio mumbled a soft, *"Si, Patron,"* he motioned for the men around him to come forward.

Lex said to his father: "Did you send Ward and Jane back to the ranch?"

Old Hyatt nodded. He was avoiding his son's gaze now; he seemed somehow different than Lex had ever known him, more withdrawn and somehow, in some disturbingly elusive way, more crafty and secretive.

"I sent them back with two of the men. I also told one of the men to head for Tucson and have a telegram sent down to the border Ranger detachment below Cerro Colorado to try an' intercept our cattle and those raiders. That's just in case they escape from us up here. Now you'n Raul ride on around the hill and . . . no. No; let's change that. Leave Raul here with the others and take Pifas with you." Old Hyatt finally looked over at Lex. "That's right," he said, reaffirming his correction. "Take Pifas with you and scout on around the hillside for the others." Hyatt turned and called over, "Pifas, fetch your horse and Lex's animal. The two of you get goin'. There's not a whole lot of daylight left."

Pifas obediently brought over the horses. As Lex mounted he saw the strange way old Jeb was regarding his father. He thought Jeb had also noticed the change in Hyatt, but that's all he thought as he and Pifas rode away through the trees.

THIRTEEN

Lex could have wished his father had not changed his original notion to have Raul Hernandez ride around the forested hillside with him, because, although Epifanio was a good man and a brave one, he quite lacked Raul's Apache instincts.

He had no idea why his father had changed companions on him at the last minute. All he knew was that old Hyatt was not acting at all normally now. That was of course understandable. With Ward murdered so senselessly, his father's grief would be deep.

Pifas picked up a set of horse-tracks, pointed them out to Lex and for a hundred yards or so they paralleled these fresh indications of horsemen. After that, though, because the forest was more dense on around the sidehill, they hid their horses and went along on foot.

Around the mountains southerly curving, shadows became deeper and cooler. Here, because sunblast didn't strike after noon, it was much more pleasant. It would be a natural place for raiders to spend the fading last daylight hours. They moved with great caution, believing that regardless of how secure the marauders felt, habit as well as ingrained prudence would have them place a sentinel somewhere around.

Epifanio halted once, where the lower-down lift and

flow of that immense desert was softly visible in the afternoon, and for a long time he did not move. He had seen something, was closely keeping track of whatever it was which had caught his attention, and when Lex glided over he pointed downward.

It was possible from Epifanio's place to see Brawley Wash, the north-to-south flow of the big desert between both flanges of the Sierritas, and even the southward country as far away as Cerro Colorado, where an adobe village lay back against the shielding foothills. They could not make out that village at all, nor did they try, for what had captured the old *vaquero's* sudden attention was the Morgan herd. It was down there in the shade of Brawley Wash not moving at all. It had come a long way through killing daytime heat; it was run-down and leg-weary. For as long as thirst did not make it edgy, it would remain exactly where it was, content to lie in the shadows.

"Tired," said Epifanio, watching that big band of quiet cattle. "Tired, *Señor,* and perhaps fifteen pounds lighter, each animal."

Lex stonily regarded the cattle. They were good animals, worth a small fortune even this far from rails-end, and yet neither he nor his father had ever considered them worth what they had thus far cost—the life of his brother.

Lex stepped back into shade, dropped to one knee, leaned upon his carbine and looked away from the cattle on through the rough-barked old pines around them. Somewhere hereabouts would be the bandits who had stolen that herd. They wouldn't be out of sight of their prize. He could imagine them idly loafing, awaiting nightfall, smoking, sipping from their canteens, playing Monte perhaps, chewing the *jarqui*—called 'jerky' by the Americans—men such as they were invariably carried with them.

Epifanio came over and sank down to rummage the onward land too. He was glum-looking and quiet for as long as they took to make sure it would be safe to slip onward another hundred yards. Then, as Lex rose up to move out, Epifanio said, "Raul would have been better at this."

Lex turned, waited for the *vaquero* to stand up, then said, "We'll make it, Pifas, you and I?"

"Yes, *Señor,* I think so. Anyway, who would want to be back there—now?"

Epifanio's voice had sounded full of gloominess. He started to edge past and had his dark eyes probing the trees when Lex's arm shot out.

"I don't understand," Lex murmured. "What's so terrible back there, Pifas?"

"What is so terrible?" echoed the pock-marked man, and rolled his eyes in that way he had of doing. "You did not make the long ride up here with your father; you wouldn't know what is so bad perhaps. Jeb knew; the others knew. Your brother's death did something to your father, *Señor.* I have served him fifteen years; I knew him; I could predict him. Not now, *Señor.* He is a different man."

Lex had vaguely felt this back there so now he

gently inclined his head. "Grief takes many forms, *amigo.*"

"Si," Epifanio quietly agreed. He kept looking straight into Lex's eyes. "But how many times does one see it turn cruel, *Señor?*"

"Cruel?"

"Yes. Why do you imagine your father sent me around this hill with you instead of Raul?"

A frightening thought began to form in Lex's mind. He stared hard at Epifanio and said nothing.

"Let me tell you, *Señor,*" went on the *vaquero.* "While we were riding up here this afternoon your father was like an avenging angel up ahead on his horse, and after Raul found us he and Raul rode ahead together and spoke quietly—so quietly the others of us heard nothing. Then, *Señor,* after wc arrived here, your father changed his mind and sent me to scout around the hill with you instead of Raul. Surely, you can understand why that was."

Lex stood like stone without looking away from Epifanio or speaking for a long while. Ultimately though, he whispered: "Why?"

"Your father meant to kill those prisoners from the moment Raul rode down to us with the news that they had been captured."

Lex swung around. Epifanio caught his arm and held on. "No, there's no point in going back. It will be all over by now. Listen, *Señor;* listen to me. I offered no objection when your father told me to accompany you; I knew that it would be better if I left with you. I could not stop him and I did not wish to remain and witness that barbarity. But I thought if anyone could prevail upon him not to do this thing, it would be Jeb. Those two have grown old together; they have been more than friends for a lot of years. In some ways your father would listen to Jeb before he would listen to you."

Epifanio dropped Lex's arm and softly shrugged. He glanced around them then back to Lex again. He leaned upon his Winchester and made that little gentle shrug again.

"Either way, *Señor,* by now it is all over."

Lex heard the quiet finality in old Epifanio's voice with grim realization that what the *vaquero* had said was true. By now it would be all over.

He dropped down again and vividly recalled the slit-eyed way Raul Hernandez had regarded those prisoners. He recalled too how Raul had shrugged off the looks of horror back in that little meadow where he'd knifed to death Ward's murderer. It was clear to him now why his father had suddenly, craftily changed his mind and sent Epifanio to scout ahead with Lex, instead of the more qualified *vaquero,* Raul Hernandez.

He recalled with sickening understanding now, that peculiarly elusive manner of his father's. Epifanio was right; Hyatt had planned to kill those three captives all along. He'd probably conspired to do it long before he even saw those raiders. He and Raul Hernandez.

Epifanio brushed Lex's shoulder lightly, saying, "*Señor,* we are wasting time. We must finish this scout."

Lex did not rise up for a while longer though, but eventually he did. Then, the pair of them continued gliding from tree to tree, from shadow to shadow, from brush clump to brush clump, until, with the solid bulk of that forested mountain squarely at their backs, they finally caught the fragrance of tobacco, and five minutes later peered through a dense copse of red-barked manzanita into a level, small glade where men stood or sat or lounged against tree-trunks, some smoking, some flat-out sleeping with sombreros over their faces, but all of those bandoleered marauders thoroughly at ease and relaxed.

"Eight," whispered Epifanio. "There must be another one or two somewhere around though. They'd have watchers posted surely."

Lex made no comment. He studied those men, and on across where lush grass grew around a marshy little seepage-spring, he also studied their horses. The animals were bridleless but saddled. Although the cinchas were visibly loose so that the animals could graze in comfort, it would still require less than a minute for the raiders to yank up latigos, yank back their bridles and spring aboard. These were seasoned outlaws, every one of them.

Lex tapped his companion and started to inch backwards. They used lots of time getting safely away from that place because Lex also felt that somewhere the marauders had sentries out. The trouble was that no matter how hawk-eyed a man was in this forested country, visibility would be definitely limited and a man would be reduced to listening for strange sounds more than watching for what might make those sounds.

When they considered themselves safely clear, Lex turned and went back towards that place where he'd left his father and the others, with thrusting, long strides. Epifanio had to scuttle swiftly on his shorter legs to keep up. When they eventually came near, Raul Hernandez suddenly and silently stepped from behind a tree to block their path. He had obviously been detailed to guard the way in. Lex halted, stared hard at Hernandez without saying a word, then brushed on by him. The next person he encountered was old Jeb. That was out a hundred yards from the others too, and while it did not occur to Lex right then that this was no chance meeting, that old Jeb had walked out here purposefully to intercept him, he peered intently into the old cowboy's face, and saw in those pale, troubled eyes what he'd hoped against hope he would not see. He halted and said, "Jeb, they're dead, aren't they?"

"Yes, they're dead, son. I figured I'd run across you first. That's why I came out here. Did you find the others?"

"We found them. They're a mile on around the mountainside. Jeb, couldn't you stop him?"

"No," said the old cowboy softly. "No one could

have stopped it, Lex. Listen to me a moment; when you walk on in don't make a fight out of it. Lex, he's not the same. Ward's death has done something to him. You go ragin' at him right now, boy, and I don't know what might happen. Anyway, son, it ain't up to you'n me to judge your paw. There's a higher authority for that."

"How did he have it done, Jeb—Raul Hernandez?"

"Only for that feller who'd been in the canyon with Ward an' Miss Jane. He turned Raul loose on that one. The other two he ordered hung. They took 'em down into a little canyon where a big oak tree grew, and yanked 'em up down there. They're still danglin' down there. Lex, leave it bc for now."

"Hell," Lex said, looking at old Jeb from dismayed eyes. "If we get the others he'll want to do the same, Jeb. There are eight or ten of them." Lex's gaze turned sardonic. "You reckon he can find enough oaks up here for that many, Jeb? I'll be damned if I'll let him do that again. I'll be damned if I will!"

"All right," soothed old Jeb. "All right, Lex. I'll stand beside you next time. But these other three—that's already done. Jumpin' him about it won't change a cussed thing. All I'm prayin' for now, Lex, is peace between you'n him. That's why I'm out here; to ask you—to plead with you—not to force him, boy. Not now, not in his present frame of mind. Ward's killin' fogged-up his mind someway. He's different; plumb different than I've ever seen him before."

"You mean crazy, don't you, Jeb?" asked Lex,

looking more sardonic than ever.

"All right, crazy then. But crazy like a wolf or a lion or a grizzly bear. Crazy-mad and plumb willin' to kill anything an' any one. He's got some notion every one of these marauders is responsible for Ward's death, an' in a way I reckon he's right. But hell, Lex, he just can't hang fourteen or fifteen men to avenge one man, can he?"

Lex shook his head and turned as Epifanio and Raul Hernandez came walking up. For a moment he and Raul looked at one another. There was nothing he could say to the lithe *vaquero.* He had expressly forbidden Hernandez to kill that particular Mexican outlaw, but Raul had been under Lex's orders only for as long as Hyatt was not there to supersede them, which Hyatt had done, so now there was nothing Lex could say.

Jeb jerked his head rearward. "The others'll be waitin' to hear," he murmured. "Let's get along now."

They returned to where the horses, the silent, wooden-faced *vaqueros,* and old Hyatt were waiting. Lex and his father exchanged a look and neither seemed willing to speak first. Epifanio stepped forth, gestured with an upflung arm, and explained where they had located the marauders and how many they were. Old Hyatt listened attentively with that uncommon look of secretive craftiness upon his normally roughly forthright and candid face. Lex looked away from him. One of the *vaqueros* came over and offered Lex a dried twist of jerky. Lex took it, thanked the cowboy, bit off a piece and started chewing. In front of him stood those two head-hung horses the prisoners had been riding when he and Raul had captured them.

He was standing slightly apart from where his father, Epifanio and Raul Hernandez were softly speaking. Old Jeb walked over to stand silently beside him. Near the horses, where the *vaqueros* philosophically endured all this, exactly as they always endured everything from rainstorms to lynchings, there was not a sound.

Dusk was beginning to form off in the places beyond their forest they could not see. It brought a steadily increasing gloominess to the uplands, making them a lonely and mournful place to be.

For some reason Lex thought of Jane Adair. What had started out to be an adventure for her had turned into a nightmare of tragedy and death. He thought of her until his father suddenly turned and called over, saying, "All right, men; let's go. We've got just about enough daylight left to do what must be done."

FOURTEEN

They left the horses, took their carbines and started up around the sloping mountainside behind Raul Hernandez. Old Hyatt paced silently along behind Raul and the others were strung out behind old Hyatt. Because of the thickening shadows it was possible to make better time now than it had been before.

They halted twice. Once, after they'd been on the trail about fifteen minutes and Raul signaled with a flung-back arm for stillness and silence while he scouted ahead. And again, part way around the hillside when they caught that first view of the Morgan herd down in Brawley Wash.

The desert was cooling off now, down there. Most of its daytime heat-haze was gone. The yonder saw-toothed peaks between where the Morgan Ranch men stood and the unseen far-away river, were delicately pink on top and darker on down their stony sides. The flat land between those two divisions of the same range was as barren, as empty and forbidding as it always was, giving to men that unique feeling that they were entirely alone in the world.

Hyatt gestured impatiently for the stalking to begin again, and it did. But now, in accordance with the plan, Raul began climbing higher up through the trees, at the same time heading on southward in a big curving arc.

Lex had no trouble understanding what his father had decided. It was basically what the old man had said right along should be their objective; get between the Mexicans and their normal southward escape route; cut them off from a dash down into Sonora where their only safety lay.

Raul kept climbing and gliding southerly, never halting and only very rarely even looking back. Once, Lex thought he caught that elusive fragrance of tobacco again. He thought they must be about parallel with the farther-down marauders, although he had not been this far west on his earlier scout with Epifanio Garcia.

Up here, a good half-mile above the marauders, there was a lingering hotness from the setting sun. In climbing to this height they had also rolled back time. As they passed through a scooped-out hollow near the top-out of this high place, they actually saw the sun once, for a brief time before they passed along back into the forest again; it was perched within inches of a great jagged spire far off upon the rim of their world. It was blood-red and huge.

Raul finally stopped, dropped to one knee and was motionless for a long time watching something dead ahead. As the others came up and also dropped down, most of them from exhaustion rather than quick interest in whatever it was Hernandez had seen, Raul turned and Lex saw that merciless grin upon his face again.

Raul leaned over, put his lips to old Hyatt's ear and whispered something. Old Hyatt reared back, squinted ahead, shrugged and nodded. Hernandez at once rose up and slipped away. As they watched him fade out through trees and shadows Jeb grunted softly at Lex's side.

"He's spotted one of their sentinels. I wouldn't want to be in that Mex's boots right now."

They sat like rocks, waiting and watching. Epifanio and the other *vaqueros* were patently on edge with this silence and its portents. They were concentrating on the reddish-hued onward forest.

From time to time it was possible to glimpse Hernandez as he moved in towards a jumble of rocks with hoary lichen on them. Sometimes he was as still as stone. Other times he slipped ahead, dropped prone or disappeared behind a tree.

None of them had, up to now, seen that marauder over in those rocks. But now they did; the Mexican stood up suddenly swinging his head left and right. He acted like a man who had just had a premonition. They could tell from the way he constantly changed position that he hadn't yet spotted Raul Hernandez, but they could also tell that the Mexican felt something wrong.

Hernandez was suddenly invisible now. They knew about where he was, or had been, but strain as they might, none of them saw him at all.

The Mexican stepped out of his rocks. He was a burly-made powerful man. He had his huge hat upon the back of his head and some greasy, dark curls of hair lay across his broad, low forehead. He held his carbine up across his body with both hands. He looked straight southward down where the men from Morgan Ranch lay hidden and scarcely breathing. From this high up, that marauder had a splendid view of the entire countryside in all directions, but closer, within a few hundred yards of him, his visibility was obstructed by the forest and the forest's increasing gloom. He stepped further away from his rocks. He was definitely troubled by something now; they could see his dark frown and his listening posture as he suddenly halted and very slowly turned his head.

Jeb whispered: "It won't be long now."

And it wasn't. Raul seemed to rise up under the sentinel's feet. One minute he was lost to them all, the next minute he was lunging for the Mexican with his knife-hand whipping inward with the hurtling weight of that lithe, panther-like body behind it.

The Mexican gasped. They all heard that. They also all heard that solid 'tunk' as Hernandez's dagger slid across the marauder's crossed bandoleers, through his chest, and struck bone.

Epifanio Garcia said almost inaudibly in Spanish: "Mother of God."

The Mexican fell with a soft-rustling sound, lost his carbine and rolled over, pushed himself up onto all fours and tried to lift his head. Raul stood above him grinning. The Mexican's elbows and knees sprung loose, he fell face down and did not move again. Raul turned as he put up his knife, still grinning, and motioned for the others to come along. Old Hyatt was the first to spring up and hike ahead. Jeb and Lex were next. Behind them came Epifanio and the shaken *vaqueros*.

In soft Spanish old Jeb said, walking along beside Lex as they passed that dead man, an old Spanish proverb: "In the land of the blind, the one-eyed are king." In English he added: "He could see everywhere but close by his hiding place. What a lousy way to die."

Hyatt caught up with Raul and those two spoke back and forth briefly, then Raul began dropping eastward down the mountainside. Jeb, seeing this, said, "Lex, are we beyond them now?"

Lex nodded but did not speak. They were a long half-mile beyond where he and Epifanio had seen those loafing raiders, of that he was positive. What he was less certain of was, with those two unpredictable leaders of theirs on ahead, what was going to happen when the fight started.

They went downhill for a long time before they finally halted again and Hernandez left them. Now, for the first time, old Hyatt strode over and halted beside Lex; he gave his oldest son that peculiarly smoky gaze Lex had noticed earlier and instead of seeming as forthright as he always had before, old Hyatt acted vague and crafty. He said, "Son, you'n Jeb drop downhill a ways. They'll make a run for it more'n likely. When you fire, concentrate on setting them afoot. If they get past us on horseback we'll never see them again." Hyatt turned, beckoned up Epifanio, and sent the *segundo* with another cowboy back up the hill to cut off the raiders, should they attempt fleeing westward. He told the remaining two *vaqueros* to drift on around the sidehill and get between the raiders and where they had left their own horses. To these men he said, "When you hear me yell for you to go bring up our animals, you move out and move fast."

When these dispositions had been made Lex said, "There are at least nine of them at that camp. You're splitting us up pretty thin."

To this the old man turned a crafty look. "We have the advantage of surprise," he said. "Raul and I will hit them first, and if we can't knock down at least five before they break an' scatter, then we'll deserve to lose them." He made a curt gesture. "You an' Jeb get goin' on down the hill now. Raul's comin' back."

Lex and Jeb started off. They passed Hernandez and he said softly to them, wearing his grin again. "Five of them are wrapped in their blankets. Four others are playing cards. I got right up among their horses. I would have cut their cinchas but one of the horses is only green-broke; that one snorted so I came away."

Lex considered Hernandez briefly as though balancing something in his mind he wished to say, but old Jeb plucked Lex's sleeve and the pair of them went on down the hill without Lex ever saying it. As they moved along through trees and shadows Jeb murmured, "Save your breath, boy. Nothing would change him an' as long as Hyatt's backin' him up, he'd just smile in your face anyway."

For a hundred yards Lex was quiet, then he looked over at the older man and said, "You never really know a man, do you, Jeb?"

"Well, not his kind you don't. Although I reckon if any of us had ever put our minds to it, we could've figured out how he'd react to being in a situation like this. Like Pifas has said: whatever a man is as a boy, he remains all his life."

"Hanging around the missions didn't change him at

all. Good thing none of those *padres* can see him now."

"Aw, those *padres* aren't so dumb, Lex. They know how it is with folks. They only do what is right; beyond that it's up to the individual."

They went down a little further before Jeb halted and looked around, his lined old face reflectively thoughtful. He seemed to have something troubling him so Lex halted there and waited. He knew Jeb very well. It would have been difficult for him not to; Jeb had been as much father and mother to Lex and Ward Morgan as their own father had been.

"Lex, Hernandez is a product of environment. He got tossed the wrong way is all, an' can't none of us change that. But he's not too important. The one I'm worryin' about is your paw. Now I've known Hyatt most of my life. I'd have bet good money I could predict what he'd do in any situation."

"And now you can't."

Jeb gloomily nodded, cocked his head in a listening position briefly, heard nothing, and looked at Lex again. "Now I can't, son. Something more'n just the killin' of your brother happened back in that little green meadow. Somethin' snapped inside your paw's head. You weren't there; you'n Raul left before we sent Ward an' Miss Jane back. You didn't see how his face changed, his eyes."

"I noticed that as soon as the lot of you got up here, Jeb. It's like he's suddenly become secretive."

"It's more'n that, son. I can't define it, but old Hyatt

just all of a sudden changed completely, and it scares me about as much as it worries me. One time I heard a man say grief can do that to folks. Well, maybe it can. But what's got me bothered is—will he change back? Because if he doesn't, Lex . . ." Old Jeb stood and shook his head, saying nothing more.

There was nothing Lex could say to comfort his old friend and adopted-parent, so he simply stood silent for a moment, then lay a hand lightly upon Jeb's arm.

"Come on; we've got our end of this thing to hold up. The others'll be in place by now, I expect."

They resumed their downhill walk, each of them in his own way gloomily concerned with something too abstract for either of them to completely comprehend. They got out into a little grassy place where, by stepping beyond this glade, they could look down and see the dark backs of the Morgan herd.

"Far enough," exclaimed Jeb, and hiked on northward to the edge of their glade. There, he stood a while listening, then beckoned to Lex, saying, as the larger and younger man walked over, "It'll bust loose pretty soon now, boy. There's somethin' I'd like to explain to you: I got nothin' against hangin' these damned outlaws, only I think it ought to be done accordin' to law. I know; I know how your paw feels. We both belong to the same old-time school o' thought about these things. But times change, Lex, whether men ever do or not. There's law in the Territory now; you can't support it at the ballot box and not support it up in these here hills. You got to go one way or another."

Lex gently smiled. What Epifanio had earlier said about his father, old Jeb McCarty and the others of their generation being harsh and cruel, was only partly correct; generally, those old-timers were also fair and practical men. Jeb was proving himself now to be as progressive as a man of his breed could be.

"You stand with me," Lex said, "and we'll maybe be able to keep a lot of men from dying up here at the end of a rope."

"It won't be easy," said Jeb gloomily. "I never before went up against Hyatt like this, and there've been other times when we didn't exactly see eye to eye."

"Both you and paw used to tell Ward and me to stand up for what we believe is right, Jeb," said Lex quietly. "It won't be easy for either of us."

They said no more on that topic, but turned to listening again. It was about time for Raul Hernandez and old Hyatt to make their attack.

Time ran on, the overhead sky became a diluted, steely blue-grey, and far down upon the desert the soft lowing of cattle drifted upwards making a peaceful, pleasant sound. In this forgotten, uninhabited uplands country the fate of nearly a dozen men was soon to be decided, but before that first gunshot sounded, shattering an age-old hush, all those men, the unsuspecting Mexicans as well as their tensed-up stalkers, had this quiet time to themselves to waste it as they wished. For some, it would be the last sweet taste of life they would know.

FIFTEEN

When the attack came it was startling. Where Lex and Jeb crouched at the northernmost edge of their little glade it sounded as though an entire company was firing. Lex recalled his father's comment about accounting for as many of the raiders as possible in the first attack and understood exactly how old Hyatt and Raul Hernandez were attempting to achieve this.

Each of those was firing his carbine as rapidly as he could lever up shells and yank the trigger. It made a breath-taking thunder of constant gunfire. But within seconds after all that firing erupted, men's outcries in frantic Spanish rose up through the wild shooting as the Sonora raiders whipped up out of their blankets or sprang to man their own weapons while screaming warnings to their companions.

Now other gunmen opened up, some from on up the hill westward, some further northward where Hyatt had sent those two *vaqueros* to take a position between the raider-camp and their own horses, and also from the little glade where the marauders were wildly fighting back. All that thunderous gunfire was deafening in this place which had only moments before been steeped in an age-old, endless silence.

Jeb glanced once over at Lex then glided down where a heavy growth of underbrush lay. Here, the old cowboy worked his way in out of sight beckoning for Lex to do the same.

But Lex stepped behind a large tree instead, and none too soon; he heard a man running towards him, raised his carbine and waited. Evidently at least one of those Mexicans had kept his head sufficiently to realize that no shots were coming in from the southward forest. Assuming incorrectly that safety lay in this direction, that *vaquero* was now fleeing through the trees as hard as he could run.

Lex sighted the Mexican once, where he suddenly halted, twisted to look back, then swung ahead and resumed his onward way. He was drawing a bead on the man when Jeb fired from within his clump of brush. The Mexican sprang high into the air, lit down with a scream and went diving for the protective bole of an immense red-barked old fir tree. He was dragging one leg; Jeb hadn't killed the man but neither had he cleanly missed.

Lex, scarcely heeding the tumult northwest of where he and Jeb were hiding, lowered his carbine to study the red-barked fir that protected that raider now. There was no way to approach that tree frontally, but given enough time he was certain he could get safely around behind the man.

Jeb fired again, knocked a big chunk of loose bark from the Mexican's tree, and dropped down out of sight as the wounded man fired back twice, levering and firing without any great attention to accurate aiming. One of those slugs whipped through the brush near Jeb but the other one sang five feet overhead and struck hard into a pine tree.

Jeb fired back, and Lex, watching this, saw what Jeb was doing. He wasn't especially trying to hit the Mexican, he was only trying to hold the man's attention. Lex had not fired yet; the raider had no idea he was facing two men, and as long as old Jeb kept him diverted, he wouldn't know this either.

Lex ducked over behind another tree, and another. He kept this up, springing from tree to tree until, with sweat tormenting him, he got around one big old pine and saw the Mexican's right side, his red-stained trouser-leg, and his hunched-forward shoulders where the marauder was concentrating upon Jeb's brush clump. He could have killed the Mexican easily with one shot, but instead of doing this he waited until Jcb fired again, watched the Mexican drop his head to return that fire, and he sprang forward swinging his carbine. The entire hillside was reverberating from all that other gunfire so the injured man had no inkling that someone was running up onto him from behind, until Lex's carbine-barrel struck down hard across his back.

The raider's gun exploded, dust and dirt jumped up twenty feet onward, and the Mexican himself was knocked ten feet ahead by that hard-swung blow. He was not knocked unconscious but his wind was gone and he lay out there in plain sight writhing and choking.

Lex caught up the man's Winchester, swung it once over his head and broke the barrel loose from the stock against a tree-trunk. He then stepped over and yanked away the marauder's holstered .45 and threw this second weapon as far down the hill as he could.

Jeb came fighting out of his thorny hiding place, walked over and impassively watched the marauder getting back his wind. Around them the forest shook with echoing gunfire.

That first bullet had passed completely through the injured Mexican's upper leg. In fact, if he had been moving just a little faster when old Jeb had fired, the raider would not have been struck at all. It was obviously a painful injury, but was in no sense likely to prove fatal.

Lex reached down, caught the outlaw by his bandoleers and jerked him to his feet. The man still had his mouth wide open and gaspingly twisted. He was getting his wind back but he acted as though that blow across the shoulders pained him much more than his wounded leg.

He was a young Mexican, Lex thought not more than perhaps twenty years old, but he had the indelible stamp of hard living in his eyes and across his face. He tried feebly to fight clear of Lex's powerful, restraining hand, found himself helpless to accomplish this and hung there in the more powerful man's grip glaring at both his captors.

"A kid," said old Jeb disgustedly, and leaned upon his gun for a moment considering their catch. He waggled his head back and forth, contempt showing in every line of him.

They dragged their captive over to a tree and trussed

his ankles with one of the marauder's bandoleers, and tied his arms above the wrists behind his back with the other bandoleer. Then Jeb pushed his wrinkled old face up close and said to the Mexican in border-Spanish, which was a very salty and graphic tongue, "You try and work those bonds loose, little rooster, and I'll come back and slit each lobe of your ears and pull your arms through them."

Jeb looked both capable and willing to do this; their prisoner stopped all straining against his lashings and watched as Lex and Jeb got back to their feet and stood a moment listening.

The fight had spread out now. Gunshots were no longer identifiable as coming from one group or the other. It seemed as though the hottest part of the fight was swirling southward, down in the direction of Jeb and Lex, but now too, there were moments of respite between gunshots. This indicated to both the listening men that the battlers had been thinned out.

Lex jerked his head and said, "Come on." He led Jeb off through the forest northwesterly, towards the loudest and most frequent source of gunfire. They didn't have far to go before a bandoleered Mexican abruptly rose up with his profile to them, fired at someone neither Jeb nor Lex could see, and abruptly dropped down again. Jeb snapped a hip-shot at that Mexican. The raider whirled with surprise and jumped on around a tree. Jeb levered off another shot to expedite the marauder's flight, then stepped behind a tree himself to punch fresh loads into his carbine.

Lex went onward from tree to tree until he saw a man's blurry shape fade out into some underbrush. He halted back from this spot and waited. Eventually that gunman rose warily up, ran a quick look around, evidently saw nothing and straightened up to his full height. Instantly, Lex caught the reflection of faint light off the brass casings in crossed bandoleers. He took a hand-rest upon his tree and called over to that Mexican.

"Drop your gun!"

The raider whipped sideways and slammed off a shot towards the sound of Lex's voice as he threw himself sideways. He had made a fatal error; Lex was calm. He was also anticipating just such a maneuver. He shot and the Sonora marauder gave a tremendous bound and lit down wildly flopping. The very brush patch he had thought would hide him, now kept his body from quite touching the ground. He died like that, skewered by a dozen tough branches, threshing out his life in diminishing quivers.

Somewhere on ahead a man cried out in Spanish. He had evidently glimpsed the death of that man hanging in the underbrush and understood that enemies were now southward too. He kept calling out for his surviving companions to change course, to retreat northward. If the other marauders heeded this they gave no indication of it, or at least Lex, listening to all that wild and sporadic gunfire, could not see that those cried-out warnings had changed anything.

He tried to locate the raider who was shouting,

failed and stealthily advanced through the trees for a closer approach to the source of all the gunfire. Once he dropped low, twisted and looked behind him. It was possible in all this confusion, for men to flank one another without knowing it. He himself had twice done this now and had no wish to have one of those desperate Sonorans do it to him. But he saw no one back there, not even old Jeb, so he started onward again.

Unexpectedly, a huge, hatless Mexican appeared dead ahead. This man was turning towards Lex, there was no close-by tree to spring behind, so Lex lit down with his legs wide-set to meet the rush of this large raider. The Mexican had a .45 in one fist but he was not firing it. In the split second before those two collided and Lex tried mightily to bring up his carbine, it occurred to him that the big Mexican's six-gun was empty, fired-out in the fighting, and that now the big man was trying desperately to get behind a tree somewhere so that he might reload. Then that Mexican saw Lex as he completed his twisting turn, and only a second before those two large men ran head-on into one another.

Something flashed through the air behind the big Mexican. Lex caught only a fragmentary glance of this object, then was staggered by that hurtling big body.

The Mexican dropped his .45, grabbed frantically for Lex's carbine with both hands, and was therefore unable to protect his face as Lex drew back his right fist, cocked it and fired it. The big Mexican roared like a bull, but whether with pain or desperation, Lex did not know. He dropped his hands from Lex's Winchester, stumbled backwards and that hurtling object Lex had briefly sighted before, struck the Mexican across the shoulders.

Lex was knocked clear as the Mexican was driven fiercely forward. He saw that someone had sprang from behind a tree to strike the big Mexican from the rear. In the fraction of a vivid second before these two fiercely straining men crashed to earth almost at his feet, Lex saw the face of Raul Hernandez. It was not grinning now; Raul was savagely intent upon riding the much larger man to the ground. He did it, but as his knife rose high the big Mexican arched his back half flinging Raul off. He whipped around, caught Raul's clothing and fired a massive fist which missed.

Lex was raising his Winchester when Raul writhed free and lunged straight at the much larger man. Those two met with powerful impact. The Mexican's mighty arms closed around Hernandez, his twisted, fierce face was savagely gloating as though this locking of those enormously powerful arms around an adversary was a particular strategy of his, then, with Lex looking on, the big Mexican's eyes suddenly sprang wide, his jaw dropped, and he made a loud bubbling groan.

Raul got an arm levered up and shoved. The big Mexican rocked back, dropped his head to gaze disbelievingly at the dagger buried to the hilt in his middle, and he closed both hands around its handle before he collapsed.

Raul whipped his head around at the sight of movement in this gloomy place, saw Lex standing there with his gun up ready to fire, and he made that wolfish grin up into Lex's face.

At that precise moment a gunshot crashed close by and while Lex stared, Raul's grin turned into a lopsided grimace. He raised both hands to his chest and fell heavily across the body of the man he had just killed.

Behind Lex a six-gun made its violent, throaty bellow. Jeb was there, his hand-gun low and bucking as he got off a second shot. A marauder stepped from behind a tree, looked in astonishment at old Jeb, and dropped his carbine, reached forth to steady himself upon the tree, and gently slid down it. The marauder who had shot Raul Hernandez and who had in turn been shot by Jeb McCarty, closed his eyes, pushed out all his breath and dropped his head forward. He had his back to the tree so he did not topple over, but he was quite dead.

Jeb stepped over, bent and caught hold of Raul Hernandez, eased him back as Lex sank to one knee watching, held the dying *vaquero* long enough for Lex to say to him, "Hernandez, hold on," then Jeb propped Raul with one of his own legs.

Raul smiled drowsily. There was a spreading, oily stain across the front of his shirt. *"Por nada,"* he whispered in Spanish, and went limp.

Jeb knelt and nodded his head. "Yeah, for nothing is right," he said to Lex. "I reckon that proves that a man dies as he lives. He said 'for nothing', meaning life isn't important, even when it was his own life."

They eased Raul Hernandez back down with his face upwards and his lithe, lean body comfortably flat. They did the same for the big Mexican Raul had knifed to death. They even took out the knife, and when Lex would have flung it away old Jeb reached forth, took the sticky thing and laid it beside Hernandez. He looked up at Lex and shrugged. "It was his. He believed in what it accomplished for him. Let him lie here with it."

SIXTEEN

The fight had swung on downhill now, southward. There was much less firing but it was still a fierce battle. As Jeb and Lex Morgan walked back out of sight behind a big tree leaving dead Raul Hernandez and that big Mexican lying there side by side, they heard a bull-like voice bellow out twice, repeating a call for horses.

"Your paw," said Jeb. "Sounded like he was south and north of us."

They moved out in the direction of old Hyatt's roar but didn't find him. Did not in fact find any of the Morgan men for a long while.

It was darker down the south slope. The sky was still duskily grey and full darkness would not arrive for some time yet, but as soon as the battlers dropped down towards the eastward desert where the cattle were, it became more difficult to see. At least visibility was more limited, although that smoky haze down here did not preclude sighting when movement occurred.

A man came quietly walking along behind Lex and Jeb. They didn't hear him at all, but once, when Lex turned to gaze back, he sighted that shadowy movement and instantly pushed old Jeb down into a brush clump.

The man kept walking along. He didn't seem particularly worried about being shot at. In fact he didn't seem to be even very concerned about the southward fight at all. He was carrying a carbine and he was hatless. Lex let him get within fifty feet of the brush clump, then rose up with his six-gun cocked and ready. The man saw Lex rise up, twisted towards him and caught his carbine in both hands.

"Hold it!" Lex growled.

The man tensed, hung like that a moment, then gradually relaxed, let his carbine sag and said, "*Chihuahua!* I thought you were one of *them.*" It was Epifanio Garcia.

Jeb eased out of the brush shaking his head. "You came 'thin an ace of meetin' your ancestors," he said disapprovingly. "What the hell you hikin' along out in the open like that for, anyway?"

Epifanio went over, looked southward, down closer to the desert where sporadic gunfire was erupting, and blew out a big sigh. "It looks like a battlefield back there," he murmured. "There can't be more than three or four of them left alive."

Lex eased off his hammer, leathered the six-gun and said, "None of them left behind us, Pifas?"

"None, *Señor,* unless you wish to count the dead."

"And our men . . . ?"

"Two hurt. They are the ones who went back for the horses." Epifanio looked up at Lex. "Your father and Raul got three of them in their blankets. They hit two more before the raiders could get out of their little clearing. It was like slaughtering sheep until those men got into the trees."

"Raul is dead," said Jeb.

Epifanio inclined his head. "I know. I walked past him back there. He and that big one who was their leader."

Lex looked around, listened a moment then jerked his head. The three of them started on down the hill again, moving carefully but swiftly. They saw no one until just before they came to the broken shale-rock slopes leading down into Brawley Wash. Here, the smell of cattle was strong. Here too, they found a loose horse which had been bridled by one of the raiders and led along this far before being abandoned. Jeb caught the beast but did not mount it. He led it on down to the final incline leading into the wash, and almost before the three of them felt level ground underfoot once more, someone on ahead in the formless gloom fired point-blank at them. Jeb gave a little astonished yelp, dropped the reins to his horse and dropped flat down. Lex and Epifanio went down too. The three of them lay quiet for a moment listening to the gunfire northward on up the wash. Then Epifanio had alone come to a shrewd decision.

At once an answering call back, but this was in English. Epifanio stood up, began beating dust off himself, and when Lex and Jeb saw the *vaquero* walk up out of the night they recognized him as one of their own. Jeb said something brusque and uncomplimentary but the cowboy was so vastly relieved to find it was friends behind him, not enemies, he only smiled at old Jeb.

They started northward up the wash. Somewhere southward they heard uneasy cattle lowing. Where they had hit the low country appeared to be at least a half-mile north of the stolen herd. Lex said it was a good thing the fight had not swirled down among the cattle or the beasts would have stampeded and run on over the line into Mexico anyway, raiders or no raiders.

There did not now seem to be so much firing on up the wash but what there was kept moving further away as though one party was in fierce pursuit of the other party. The more they hastened the less they appeared to close the gap until, quite unexpectedly, there was a sudden cessation altogether. Then they trotted ahead, but cautiously, each of them straining to see through the descending dusk.

Lex was out in front when something pale loomed

ahead in his path. He slowed to a careful walk, drew his hand-gun and halted five feet off. A voice in faint Spanish said, *"Por favor, Señores, no mas. No mas."*

Lex stepped up closer and dropped down. The others also sank down. It was a bandoleered Mexican lying there. He had a dark and spreading stain high and to the right. He kept faintly murmuring, *"no mas, Señores, no mas."*

"All right," Lex answered. "No more; you're safe for now. Lie still and be quiet." He bent to examine the Mexican's wound. It was a bad one but unlikely to prove fatal if treated before the man bled out. He reared back on his heels, said to the *vaquero,* "Stay with this one. Find his guns and bandage him. Check for a knife," then stood up and jerked his head at Epifanio and Jeb. Those three passed on around the two men and hurried ahead. They could now see little onward crimson flashes where the gunfire was resuming once more.

There was a landslide ahead which shone ghostly in the murky gloom. From behind this pile of tumbled stone and earth at least three men were firing southward. When a blind bullet sang close old Jeb grunted and skipped sideways. Lex and Epifanio did the same. They came up closer, saw where other men were crouching behind rocks in front of the slide and halted for Lex to call out.

As Lex opened his mouth to yell ahead that gunfire from beyond the landslide suddenly swelled and thundered making it impossible for anyone to be heard.

Lex motioned for the others to remain back where they were and ran in a low crouch towards one particular boulder where a prone man was firing with a Winchester. This man was bareheaded and in the faint light pale hair shone. Of all the men at this place only two did not have black hair; Lex and old Hyatt.

Lex got in behind that man and was starting to drop down when something the other man heard or sensed made him whip around swinging his gun as he did this. Lex saw the carbine coming and with no time to identify himself, aimed a kick. The impact of his boot-toe against solid steel sent a sharp stab of pain all the way up through his body.

"It's Lex," he exclaimed, as he dropped down beside old Hyatt.

His father's face was twisted and streaked with dirt and sweat. He made a lunge for Lex before it fully dawned upon him who Lex was, then he stopped twisting and glared upwards. "You fool," he gasped. "You could've gotten yourself killed."

Lex let that go by and peered around the boulder towards those winking muzzleblasts beyond the slide. "How many are over there?" he asked.

"Three, I think."

"Is that all that's left?"

Old Hyatt vigorously nodded and pushed his carbine around to fire again. He tugged off a shot, levered his carbine, looked down at it suddenly and put the weapon aside. It was empty. As he fumbled for his six-gun old Hyatt said, "Where the hell are the others—

Pifas an' Jeb an' Raul?"

"Pifas and Jeb are with me. They're back a little ways."

"Well, confound it, tell them to get up here!"

"And Raul is dead."

The older man raised his eyes. "Dead? Raul Hernandez?" This seemed to strike him hard. He kept looking up at Lex as though trying to grasp the finality of Hernandez's passing.

Lex turned and called back for Jeb and Epifanio to come up. They did, running zig-zaggedly forward. When they also dropped down Hyatt squinted over at them. They both woodenly returned his stare and until Lex spoke again, there was strong silence behind the boulder.

"Jeb and I'll get around behind that slide," Lex told his father. "You and Pifas and the others keep their attention down here on you."

Old Hyatt ripped out a hard curse. "Never mind takin' the risk," he said. "We'll smoke 'em out right here."

"They'll fall back," retorted Lex. "As long as they can keep that slide between us, they can fall back and maybe get away."

"Away where?" demanded Hyatt, and made a big sweep with one hand. "They're afoot and pretty soon now our horses will come up. There's nothing but open country from here on. Where could they get away to?"

"Up there," growled Jeb, and pointed back up the

mountainside. "An' I don't feel like enough of a mountain-goat to go climbin' back up there again, either. Let's do it Lex's way, Hyatt."

"You'll do it my way!" exploded the old man, his milky gaze turning fiercely upon Jeb.

Lex scowled at his father. Epifanio averted his face, turned to considering the *vaqueros* who were down here with Hyatt also firing towards the surviving marauders from behind other close-by boulders.

Jeb did not lower his eyes. He and Hyatt steadily regarded one another for a long while. Lex broke that exhibition of stubbornness by saying, "Are we fighting the raiders or each other? Listen to me, both of you; I'm going up the hill and come in behind those men. You keep their attention on you."

He started away. Old Hyatt reared up stiffly as though to lunge at Lex or to curse him, but Jeb happened to also move at the same time. Those two old men bumped, Hyatt was pushed off-balance, and before he could recover Lex was gone. Hyatt's lips parted; he ripped out a savage oath, but Jeb was firing around their protective boulder along with Epifanio, and Hyatt's epithets were drowned out very effectively.

For a while the battle swelled again towards a furious crescendo. The overhead sky was beginning now to lose its last vestiges of dusk. There was a fringe of increasing darkness above the peaks and out along the remote horizon. This lent a more solid background to those lashing tongues of flame where men fired at one another, but it also made targets more difficult to see, so the shooters concentrated upon one another's muzzleblasts.

Where Lex had left his father and the other men from Morgan Ranch, this gunfire never seemed to slacken. Bullets struck stone and screamed off into the descending night making a chilling sound. Once, Jeb and Epifanio looked over at one another above Hyatt's prone form. Without saying it they were sharing an identical thought: Lex could be killed by friendly guns in this savage battle as readily as by enemy guns. By now he would be somewhere northward of that landslide and westerly, up the sidehill. Still, the best way they could help him was by throwing lead over into that jumble of rock beyond which the last of the marauders were firing back.

Over the bedlam of gunfire a man's voice rang out somewhere beyond the slide. At once the men of Morgan Ranch ceased firing. Moments later the besieged raiders also held off. Through the sudden, crushing silence which now ensued that same powerful voice cried out again. It was Lex out there in the gloom somewhere, well behind those forted-up Mexicans, and he was calling upon them in Spanish to surrender.

For a while Lex's voice was the only sound. Then one of the marauders shouted defiance and snapped off a rearward shot. Old Jeb sprang straight up and fiercely swore at that raider. He was lifting his .45 when Lex called down to that raider that he hadn't even been close, but if he tried that again Lex would shoot him; that he could plainly see the raiders where they lay flat against their rocky bulwark.

For a long while there was not a sound from beyond the slide. During this tense interval a different sound intruded. Horses could distinctly be heard approaching from the south. Old Hyatt reared up, cocked his head, then said, "Good; the men are bringing up our animals. Just in time too."

But on across the landslide the surviving Mexicans thought that was something else; it sounded to them as though reinforcements were arriving for their attackers. They held a very brief discussion, when one of them called over to Lex that if he and his friends would not shoot them, they would throw down their guns and surrender.

Lex gave his word they would not be shot down.

A moment later one bandoleered Mexican scrambled atop his landslide and straightened up over there in full view of old Hyatt and the others. He was not shot at. Two more bandoleered raiders came up atop the slide and stood beside the first one.

Jeb got up off the boulder he'd been leaning against, walked around it and started forward. "Come down off there," he ordered as he went closer. The three Mexicans saw him and started downward towards him. Behind old Jeb, Hyatt, Epifanio, and the *vaqueros* also rose up from their hiding places. Each of them kept a cocked gun upon the surrendering marauders.

Lex came scrambling on around the slide too, and struck out towards Jeb and the captives. He alone of the victors did not have his gun drawn.

SEVENTEEN

The three Mexicans, all that remained active from an original force of ten men, were scratched and filthy from their long retreat through underbrush, over sharp-edged rocks, and among rough-barked pines and firs. They were also down to their last handful of bullets for their six-guns and each of them had long since abandoned their carbines.

Even if Lex hadn't flanked them, they couldn't have fought on much longer. As they were disarmed these three men studied their captors. They said nothing and seemed exhausted.

They were herded along ahead of the men from the Morgan Ranch until, where those two *vaqueros* loomed up holding the horses, old Hyatt called a halt. He seemed absorbed in the prisoners and even when Lex and Jeb went among the men to see who had been injured and who had not, Hyatt never stopped watching the prisoners.

Two *vaqueros,* the men who had brought up the saddle animals, were the only Morgan men who had been wounded, which in itself was some kind of a minor miracle; enough lead had been thrown in the fight to inadvertently maim more than just two men, and except for the denseness of that uplands forest undoubtedly more than two would have been hit.

Those two men were not seriously injured. One had a perforated left hand, the other had the lobe of his right ear torn and mangled, but not by a bullet, by a rigid piece of pine-limb sent arrow-straight by a ricocheting bullet.

"One man's missing," pronounced Hyatt, peering around.

Lex explained: "We found a wounded raider back a ways and left one of the *vaqueros* to patch him up."

Old Hyatt's bushy brows dropped darkly down. "Patch him up," he throatily exclaimed. "Shoot him, dammit. Don't patch any of them up—shoot them."

Lex did not comment. He and Jeb and Epifanio exchanged a look and Lex said, "We'd better build a fire, and one of us ought to go back up and fetch down the wounded—if there are any—and the prisoners."

Epifanio volunteered to go. Before Hyatt could assent or disagree Pifas took one of the other *vaqueros* and walked off. Lex called after him to see if the marauders' horses had any food in the packs, if they did have to fetch it along. Epifanio said that he would, and faded out in the thickening night.

Two *vaqueros* wordlessly turned to gather faggots for a fire. They went shuffling over towards the wash's westernmost slopes where underbrush and even an occasional stunted pine tree grew.

Jeb gazed at their captives. "Rough fight," he said to them in English. "You boys thought you'd got away clean, didn't you?"

One of the Mexicans spread his hands. "*No sabe,*" he said.

Jeb started to say the same thing over again in Spanish but Hyatt cut across his forming words. In Spanish Hyatt said, "That big one—he was your chieftain?"

"Si, Señor; el pistolero."

"The gunfighter," growled old Hyatt in strong scorn. "Pretty fancy name for a man who couldn't even protect himself, let alone his companions. You know what's going to happen to you?"

The Mexican lifted his shoulders and let them fall. He knew what would happen in Mexico, if the three of them had been taken like this down there, but he seemed unsure about his fate north of the border.

Old Hyatt lifted a hand, stretched his forefinger and drew it slowly across his own throat with unmistakable meaning. One of the other raiders, an older man with a hint of grey above his ears, looked Hyatt straight in the eye and said in quiet Spanish, "Sometimes, *Señor Jefe,* a man has a chance, and sometimes he does not. Life is a matter of taking chances and it ends for us all when we finally take the chance which does not really exist—so we die. It will be the same for you some day. Now, it is our turn."

Jeb stared hard at that one. So did Lex.

The two *vaqueros* returned with armloads of faggots, knelt and wordlessly began kindling a small fire. For a little while this seemed to hold the attention of everyone excepting old Hyatt. He was intently regarding the prisoners.

Lex and Jeb strolled down where the horses patiently stood, halted over them, and made a silent examination of the animals. There were a few bruises from rocks, a few scratches from spiny sage or buck-brush limbs, but otherwise their gaunted animals were in good shape.

"It'll be a long, hot ride back," said Jeb, when he and Lex came together again in front of the horses. "I suppose someone ought to drift on down and look at the cattle."

"They'll be all right until morning," murmured Lex, standing slouched and relaxed and gazing on ahead where his father and the prisoners were. "Maybe when Epifanio gets back he'll go have a look. Jeb?"

"Yeah."

"He's goin' to try it."

Jeb looked around then back again. He said, "Yeah," and bit that one word off.

"You still goin' to stand with me when he does try it?"

"To the hilt, boy. To the hilt. But with Raul gone I don't think he'll make any attempt to have them killed before sunup." Jeb cleared his throat of rockdust and spat. "Maybe we can pass around among the *vaqueros* and tell them not to obey him."

"No. Let's not get them involved. It'll be just you'n me against him. It's better that way."

"I reckon it is at that. Still, I'll have a word with Pifas. I'll have him tell the men not to interfere if there's a fight amongst us."

Lex nodded in agreement and the pair of them returned to the fire. There wasn't much said for a long while. When Epifanio returned with the Mexican horses he had with him two more captives. One was the youth Lex and Jeb had left tied with his own bandoleers. The second captive was that wounded man they had stumbled upon down in the southward wash. For a little while it diverted everyone, caring for the injuries of these two.

Epifanio had found some raw coffee, half ground and bitter as gall, in the outfits of one of the dead marauders. They boiled this and shared it. One of the English-speaking prisoners, over his cup of coffee, explained why they had stolen the Morgan cattle, and the way he said it made some of the Morgan men thoughtful.

"In my country there is a war going on, which is not in itself unusual, *Señores;* we often have wars. But because of this particular war there is much hunger, much famine. We were taking the cattle to our people to keep them from starving."

"Very noble," said old Hyatt bitterly. "If you'd wanted beef to prevent starvation you could have come and asked for it, and for that purpose none of the cowmen of Arizona would have refused you."

"Ah, *Señor,*" said that same, graying outlaw with a soft gaze over at old Hyatt's savage face. "You would have refused. We have asked before. Always we are told that it is the concern of the Mexican Government, not the cowmen of Arizona, to care for the people of Province Sonora."

Hyatt said no more on that topic. He glared at the marauder without speaking for a while, then he said in a soft, roughened voice, "To hell with the cattle, you thievin' whelp; you murdered my son."

The Mexican gazed long into their little fire before he finally said, "No, *Señor,* it was not I. Even our chieftain refused to hold your boy and the lovely *Señorita* prisoner. He argued with the others—and yet, *Señores,* he needed those men, for without them we could never have got all those cattle over the line into Sonora. So, he let them go and try getting ransom, providing that they would afterwards meet us down here and help us with the herd. For him, *Señores,* there was no other way." The raider raised his head, swung and looked straight at old Hyatt. "All those abductors are dead. You have had your revenge; you have killed every one of them."

"Yes," replied old Hyatt, "and in the morning when first light comes, I'll kill every one of you, too."

Hyatt rose up and walked stiffly off into the settled night. For a while they all listened to his diminishing footfalls, then Lex and Jeb looked at one another.

Epifanio Garcia, seeing the look pass between these two, said in a near-whisper, "Why isn't he satisfied with his vengeance? Why must he go on killing when the fight is ended and the chase is over?"

Lex put both hands flat down upon the earth, pushed himself upright and said, "Pifas, keep the *vaqueros* here. No matter what you hear or see, keep them here. Understand?"

Epifanio rolled his eyes at the look upon Lex's face. "They will stay here," he murmured. "Lex, be very careful. He is not your father tonight—he is someone altogether different."

Jeb also rose up, but Lex shook his head, saying, "Let me try it alone first, Jeb. You stay here and keep an eye on the prisoners."

Jeb settled back down. He said nothing. Neither did any of the others; as Lex hiked on out into the night after his father they solemnly watched him go for as long as they could discern him in the pre-moonlight gloom.

Hyatt was over by the landslide sitting atop a shattered boulder, his gauntness stark-etched in the night, his oddly altered look more pronounced than ever. He seemed withdrawn, and in fact he didn't recognize Lex until the equally as big and stout-muscled younger man halted directly in front of him and said, "Father."

Hyatt lifted his shaggy head, blinked at his remaining son and inclined his head. "We'll hang them at sunup," he said.

"We won't hang them at all, Paw."

"What?"

"I said we won't hang them at all."

Old Hyatt put that oddly milky stare back upwards again. For a moment he simply sat there on his broken boulder studying Lex's face. He had no particular expression either across his features or in his eyes while he did this, but gradually his rawboned, broad shoulders pulled up, and his long mouth drew out thin and flat against his teeth. He got up slowly off his granite rock and took one step forward. When he stopped moving he was face to face with Lex.

"Did you say we wouldn't hang them, Lex?" he demanded in a deep, gruff way.

"That's exactly what I said, Paw."

"You? You givin' me orders? You, tryin' to save the mangy hides of those murderin', thievin' greasers?"

"No, I'm not tryin' to keep them from facing justice, Paw. I just don't believe your kind of justice is right. The law'll handle those Mexicans. We won't do it your way, with hard-twist riatas tossed over oak limbs. Not this time."

Old Hyatt's face twisted with disbelief, with perplexity. He kept staring hard at his son as though trying to fathom something. He said, "Not two hours ago you were tryin' to kill those raiders, along with the rest of us. Now you're on their side."

"I'm not on their side at all, and as for fightin' them, that was entirely different; they had guns in their hands then, Paw. It was kill or be killed. But now that's finished; they're unarmed and they are our prisoners. You don't fight men who can't fight back."

Hyatt stepped backward. His expression got that odd craftiness to it again. He made a cold smile and dropped his right hand to within inches of his holstered gun. "I'm goin' to avenge your brother, Lex, an' you nor anyone else is goin' to interfere with that."

Lex saw the old man's hand edge surreptitiously closer to the saw-handle butt of his .45. He didn't wait; he balanced forward on the balls of his feet, struck at that set of curled fingers, knocked his father's hand away from the gun and started to speak. But the old man was tight-wound and exploded the moment Lex interfered with his draw. He launched himself at his son with a roar of wild wrath. Lex tried to get clear and failed. The old man's mighty arms caught him in a bear-hug. Lex had one hand, his right, free of that encircling grip. He raised it, caught the old man under the chin and with the heel of his palm threw his weight into forcing his father's head back.

There was not a sound except for the abrasive rustle of booted feet scuffling in the dust. The old man's head went unnaturally far back. His grip loosened around Lex's middle, it broke finally as Hyatt staggered clear.

Lex went in close again. Old Hyatt made a wild grab for his .45. Lex struck his father in the right shoulder half-turning him away, forcing that right hand to flounder in its purposeful downward sweep. Hyatt let off a roar, swung back and went after Lex with his big fists. He walked head-on into a jolting left over the heart, a sledge-hammer right that crunched against his jaw, and stopped dead-still with his eyes turning dull, turning milky.

Lex fired one more blow and old Hyatt went over backwards into the rocks. His head struck the boulder he'd earlier been seated upon with a sickening sound and he crumpled off to one side.

Behind Lex someone gasped. Old Jeb darted past, got down beside Hyatt and lifted his head. "Hit the damned rock," he said breathlessly. "Lex, fetch some water and a blanket. He's out cold."

Back at the little fire those swarthy, dark men, guards and captives alive, were wooden-faced and totally silent. They had seen that quick, fierce scuffle, that unexpectedly damaging fall; it held them in shocked stillness now.

Lex got a blanket and a canteen, returned to where old Jeb was worriedly squatting, and silently, deftly made a pillow for his father's head from the blanket, and handed Jeb the water. Hyatt's breathing was fluttery, his face was grey as death.

EIGHTEEN

They made old Hyatt as comfortable as they could. Over at the fire Epifanio passed out more coffee, ordered the captives tied when they had drunk their fill, and took the first watch as the marauders and the Morgan Ranch *vaqueros* lay back to sleep.

Over head, the big old yellow moon came silently gliding. It was a warm, balmy night. Once, along towards midnight, one of their horses nickered, which brought drowsing Epifanio Garcia to his feet with his carbine up and ready. But the sound was not repeated, so when old Jeb walked over to listen, Epifanio made a little apologetic shrug and said, "A man's nerves crawl like white worms sometimes."

Lex and Jeb came to the fire. They had made old Hyatt as comfortable as they could. They had bathed his face and covered him with a second blanket. Beyond that there was nothing they could do until he roused out of his coma.

"I had no idea he'd strike that rock," murmured Lex.

"Of course you didn't," muttered old Jeb. "And you were plumb right in what you were tryin' to do. Don't blame yourself, son."

"It sounded like his skull busted, Jeb."

"Naw. Nothing's busted, boy. It was just one hell of a hard bump is all."

"Are you sure?"

Jeb sidestepped answering by holding up a freshly filled tin cup. "Here, guzzle some of this lye-water. I never could understand how the Mexicans could drink this stuff. It's more like embalmin' fluid than coffee."

Lex drank. He was so tired his mind wasn't working properly. Even that terrible coffee didn't keep him from sagging, and finally, sitting cross-legged, to fall asleep.

Jeb and old Epifanio looked soberly at Lex, then at one another. The *segundo* said softly, "It looked bad from where I sat."

"It was bad," whispered Jeb. "Anyone with a thinner skull would have had their danged head busted like a rotten melon, Pifas. Go over an' sit by him, will you; I'm goin' to walk out a little ways."

"You heard something out there?" asked Epifanio, suddenly wide awake.

Jeb rose up shaking his head. "Just want to be alone for a little while," he mumbled, and walked off in the direction of their horses.

Moonlight shone softly against the grey-slack faces of the slumbering men. It also shone off the saddled, bridleless horses on down the wash where they nibbled at short stalks of withered grass. Elsewhere, that soft, golden light lay up along the gloomy hillside to the west, and out over an enormous expanse of emptiness to the north, east, and south.

Old Jeb, weary in body and spirit, watched the horses a while, sauntered southward among them, halted and made a brown-paper cigarette. He lit up behind his hat to hide the match-flare and he afterwards mightily exhaled, cocked his head back and gazed up at the curving sky. He was standing like that when a quiet, low voice spoke to him from a distance of no more than a hundred feet rearward, turning Jeb to stone.

"Steady, mister, steady now. What the hell's goin' on up here?"

Jeb neither answered that foreign voice nor moved a muscle. He heard soft footfalls approaching from the rear and waited. Whoever that was out there in the night had craftily used the horses to hide behind. He wasn't a Mexican; his drawl had been pure Southwest. Then the stranger halted and said, "Face around, mister, but do it easy-like."

Jeb obeyed; he kept his right hand clear of his holster too, and found himself gazing at a lean, lantern-jawed, rough looking man with the badge of an Arizona Ranger upon his shirt-front. Jeb let off an audible sigh of strong relief.

"At my age," he said to the Ranger dryly, "a feller can't afford to get scairt out of ten years of his life. How'n hell'd you ever sneak up on me like this?"

The Ranger made a little smile. "While back one of the cussed horses snickered," he said. "I thought sure we were goners when that happened."

"We?"

The lantern-jawed man made a rearward gesture. "Seventeen of us around you, mister. We got the word from folks who'd seen gunflashes up the hill, couple hours back, that there was a big fight goin' on out here."

"Where you from, Ranger?"

"Cerro Colorado. Are you the Morgan outfit?"

Jeb dropped his smoke and stepped on it as he bobbed his head up and down. "Yeah. We're the Morgan outfit. An' we got us some Mex raiders who ran off our cattle and—"

"Killed old Hyatt Morgan's youngest boy," said the Ranger, breaking across Jeb's muttered words.

"How'd you know that?"

"We got a young lady with us, mister. She hit the trail south from Tucson, got to our barracks just as we were ridin' out."

"Jane Adair?"

"The same."

"Where?" demanded old Jeb. "By gawd, Ranger, that girl's got more guts than ten men, if she made that ride after all she's been through."

"Well," said the Ranger, "you go on back to your camp an' pass the word that we're comin' in, so no one gets edgy and tries to pot-shoot us, and I'll fetch her along with the rest of my crew. All right?"

"Sure," said Jeb swiftly, and emphatically bobbed his head up and down. "All right." He turned and hurried back northward with the dying coals of their little cherry-red fire to guide him.

He burst upon the camp crying out that Arizona Rangers were around them in the night and succeeded in bringing everyone whirling up off the ground, even the prisoners. Epifanio came running over from his vigil beside old Hyatt and when he tried to say something to Lex, the younger man brushed him aside as he sprang over to question Jeb.

While this excitement and confusion was at its height someone halloed from out beyond the fire-circle, and old Jeb halloed right back that it was all right for the Rangers to walk on in.

They did, all seventeen of them; lean, sinewy men bristling with guns. Where they halted that same lantern-jawed man introduced himself as Captain Seth Piper. When Jeb had introduced Lex, Epifanio and himself, Captain Piper said laconically, "We found your herd bedded down, southward a ways. Looks like the raiders darn near got over the line with 'em."

From over by the landslide a man's garrulous, unsteady voice bleated audibly, and as Lex spun towards that sound Epifanio said at his elbow, "That's what I've been trying to tell you; your father has regained consciousness."

Lex walked away from the others. They scarcely missed him, for as he turned his back Jane Adair rode up on a big black horse, stepped down and caught the attention of every man there except Lex. Old Jeb went over to her waggling his head.

"You shouldn't have," he said, taking one of the lovely girl's hands and tightly holding it. "Ma'am, you should've stayed in Tucson and rested up."

She smiled into old Jeb's eyes completely melting him with her warmth and her gentle strength. "I had to, Jeb. I knew what Mister Morgan expected of me; I had to prove to him that—"

"Ma'am," Jeb cut in to fiercely say, "you don't have to prove nothin' to anyone of us. No, sir, you don't. I told Hyatt an' Lex the first day out you were as much man as either of them were, by golly."

"Is Lex all right, Jeb?"

"Fine, ma'am. He's fine. He's—uh—well, I reckon he's over with his paw right this minute but he's—"

"Did something happen to Mister Morgan, Jeb?"

"Well, yes, ma'am, it did. You see—"

Epifanio stepped up and broadly smiled. He said, "*Señorita, el jefe* had a small accident. He tripped and struck his head on a rock. But it will be all right now."

Jeb looked gratefully around at the *segundo* and

bobbed his head up and down again. "That's exactly what happened, ma'am. Old Hyatt bumped his head."

"Where?" asked Jane, and when Epifanio pointed northward towards the landslide she left her horse and walked in that direction.

The Ranger officer, returning from a look at the captives, stepped in front of Jeb and Epifanio, threw a skeptical look up the westward mountain and shook his head. "Must've been quite a battle," he mused. "They tell me there are dead ones scattered all the way up to the top."

Jeb suddenly gave a start. He had just remembered those three hanged marauders. "In the morning," he said quickly, "we'll go up there with you and help fetch 'em back down here." He nervously smiled. "Say, you don't happen to have any decent coffee along, do you?"

The officer gravely inclined his head at Jeb. He seemed to be a particularly astute man, for after he'd sent one of his rangers for their packs, he said, "Tell me, Mister McCarty, how many of the raiders got tangled up in their own ropes and committed suicide?"

"Suicide, Captain? I don't know what you're talkin' about."

The lantern-jawed ranger rubbed his scratchy jaw and steadily regarded old Jeb for a moment before he slowly dropped one lid over one eye, and slowly raised the lid. "Some of your *vaqueros,*" he murmured softly, "been answerin' our questions. Seems they were standin' there in a clump of oak trees when a couple of those marauders got hanged—hanged themselves I mean, Mister McCarty. Sure too bad, isn't it; still, it saves the Territory of Arizona two expensive court trials, so I reckon it's better this way."

Epifanio was grinning. Jeb though, didn't look so relieved until he'd asked the lanky, lean ranger officer one question. "Captain, if a man's out of his head when he does somethin', does the law figure he's responsible?"

Captain Piper shook his head. "No. But don't worry about it anyway. Your *vaqueros* won't talk and neither will my men. But even if they did, no one would ever be brought to trial for hangin' marauders from south of the border. You couldn't get an unfavorable jury in southern Arizona if you turned over every rock tryin'."

Someone was calling Jeb's name from beyond the fire. Epifanio touched Jeb's arm and said, "Lex wants you over by the landslide. You go; I'll build up the fire and make fresh coffee."

Jeb went. He strode through the crowd of armed men looking ahead where Lex and Jane Adair had propped old Hyatt up against the same shattered old boulder he'd hit his head upon. As he halted, sank down to one knee and gazed at Hyatt, his eyes troubled and uncertain, Lex's father lifted his head. His eyes were as clear, as forthright as they'd ever been. He shoved out a big hand towards Jeb.

"Glad to see you're all right," Hyatt said, in the same old gruff, candid voice Jeb had known for so many years. "I got to apologize, though, Jeb, if I wasn't much good in the fight. Somethin' happened; I don't know exactly how to explain it. I can't remember very much of what happened between the time we saw Ward get killed and right now. It's all sort of vague. Reckon maybe the sun got to me, Jeb. I'm sorry."

"Sorry," exclaimed Jeb, grasping Hyatt's hand and vigorously pumping it. "Sorry. Hell's bells, Hyatt, you done just right. You'n Lex both. And Miss Jane here; you know what she did after she got back?"

"Yes, I know. Let go my hand you old fool. I got a splittin' headache and all that pumpin' doesn't help it one cussed bit."

Jeb looked down, seemed surprised to find himself holding Hyatt's paw, and dropped it. He smiled; his face broke up into serrated ridges and lines. "They're makin' some decent coffee," he said, getting back upright again. "I'll go fetch us some."

Hyatt smiled. "You do that, Jeb. You do that." He rolled his head sideways where Lex and Jane Adair were standing. "Why don't you two walk on down an' check the horses for us?" he asked.

Jeb, in the act of moving off, twisted and called back. "I already checked 'em, Hyatt. They're just fine."

"You," growled old Hyatt, "just fetch that cussed coffee and mind your own business."

Jeb chuckled. "Just like always," he said, and went prancing happily back towards the fire. "Must've been that bump on the head fetched him back to normal."

Hyatt watched old Jeb leave with a soft twinkle in his eyes. Still watching Jeb, he repeated to Lex and Jane Adair what he'd said earlier about checking the horses. Then, as those two moved slowly off side by side, he turned his attention upon them. He heard Lex say something and saw Jane turn to look at Lex's profile before she answered.

"It wasn't so bad, Lex. I learned something on that ride from Tucson to Cerro Colorado."

"What was that, ma'am?"

"Exhaustion consists of two parts of tiredness. First, you have to be weary in body. I was that, all right. But secondly, you have to also be tired in the spirit—in the heart and mind. And that's what I wasn't."

"No?" said Lex, as they passed out around all those milling men around the campfire. "Why not?"

"I was too worried about the rest of you. About what might happen when you caught the marauders."

Ahead of them the horses loomed up, some still browsing but most of them standing hip-shot and drowsing under that huge old yellow moon.

Lex halted and faced around. Where golden light touched Jane's dark russet hair it made a soft pattern. Her gaze was somber and unwavering as she returned his look.

"When we get back," he quietly said, "and all this is more or less forgotten . . ."

"Yes, Lex?"

"I'd like to bring you out to the ranch again, Jane. To

show you how things are normally, at our place. Maybe to tell you how you affected me that night when we all had supper together."

"I'd like that, Lex. I'd like it very much."

They stood a moment gazing straight at each other, then Lex turned a little and stared down the southward night where the Morgan herd was bedded down, where Mexico lay further southward.

Over in the quiet east where moonlight struck the Sierritas, a rich softness lay which made this a very special night to that man and the girl there with him.

He reached for her fingers, found them, and gently squeezed them. She returned his grip, freed her fingers and they turned to slow-pace their way back towards the little fire with its delicious aroma of fresh-boiling coffee.

Center Point Publishing
600 Brooks Road • PO Box 1
Thorndike ME 04986-0001 USA

(207) 568-3717

US & Canada:
1 800 929-9108